MW00936151

A
Charming
Secret

A Magical Cure Mystery

Book Six

Acknowledgements

I have a whole bunch of people to thank for the love of this ongoing series. June Heal and the gang holds a special place in my heart. She allows us to become someone who is courageous, fun, and witchy. She lets us escape from the everyday life into a fantasy we would all like to be.

My fabulous readers keep her alive and for that I am grateful! Thank you, Susan Parham, for coming up with a fun truth potion to add to A Charming Secret. June was able to solve the case because of you!

Happy reading! I hope you come back to Whispering Falls for a longer visit!

Chapter One

"Mr. Prince Charming?" I fanned the smoke trying to clear a path in front of me. Nothing but darkness lay ahead. The sounds of crackles rang in my ear. The uneasy feeling poked my gut, sending a sick feeling to my stomach. My intuition telling me something was wrong. Something evil was surrounding me. Frantically, my eyes scanned for a sighting of my cat's white tail. I screamed, "Mr. Prince Charming!"

Fear knotted my insides. The thick heavy black soot filled my lungs. The crackle of the fire was getting louder. The structure around me groaned as though it was telling me it was giving up. Caving in. For a second the smoke lifted around me. Mr. Prince Charming's tail danced in the air off in the distance.

"Mr. Prince Charming! No!" I screamed sensing the danger.

A loud crack above me was deafening. I covered my arms over my head and dropped to the floor right before the burning beam came crashing down, barely missing me. My eyes slid across the floor. There was an inch above the ground where the smoke hadn't touched, though I was unable to escape the heat. The hairs on my arms sizzled as the temperature rose around me.

A bright yellow glow illuminated in front of me. My eyes darted in that direction. "Madame Torres," I whispered reaching out to my crystal ball.

Madame Torres was more than an arm's reach away. She glowed as bright as fire. Swirls of red, yellow, blue, and purple took up all of her glass ball.

"Help me," I begged, coughing the words out of my mouth. My fingers inched toward her. Reaching, reaching, reaching, but she was too far.

Loyal, true, trustworthy, unwavering. *The black words flashed in bold in her ball.*

"No!" I rolled to my side as I watched the fire creep onto my fingertips, covering me like a snake, coiling

around my arms, around my legs, my torso, all over my body, choking the life out of me.

"It's okay," the familiar sound of Oscar Park woke me up along with his hand caressing my hair. "It's just a dream."

I gasped for air, sitting straight up in the bed, flinging him off me.

"Where is he?" My eyes darted around the bedroom of my little cottage, searching for my fairy-god cat. I patted my body realizing I was not burnt to a crisp. "Mr. Prince Charming!"

Mewl. My furry, solid white feline lifted his head from his curled position at the edge of my bed. He yawned before nesting his head upside down to continue his night's sleep.

I burst out in tears.

"It's okay." Oscar pulled me closer trying to calm me in the midnight hours. His black hair gleamed in the moonlight that was darting through the window. "It's okay." His voice faded to a hushed stillness, making me feel somewhat better.

I looked into his blue eyes, so comforting. I ran my finger over my left ring finger where my mother's wedding ring had found a home when Oscar had asked me to marry him.

"Are you okay?" he asked.

I nodded my head and glanced out at the full moon. Something told me it wasn't going to be all right.

Chapter Two

Oscar was long gone before I got up to get ready to head down the hill toward A Charming Cure, my homeopathic cure shop in our magical village of Whispering Falls, Kentucky.

To the world, Whispering Falls was just another town on the map with cute, eclectic shops with unique gifts and gift ideas. Whispering Falls was much more than that. So much more.

The town I had called my home for a couple years now was magical. Every shop owner had a spiritual talent the mere mortal couldn't comprehend. Thanks to my father's side of the family, I had the gift of intuition.

It came in especially handy in my potion shop. Not all the time, but most of the time a customer came to my shop for a homeopathic cure, when in reality they need a little dose of magic added—life instead of the cure for heartburn, they needed my love potion to set their life back into motion.

Harmless. Good witch sort of things. Technically I was a Good-Sider witch. Only we didn't call ourselves witches, we were spiritualists. We uplifted people's spirits.

"Are you ready?" I asked Mr. Prince Charming as I took one last look in the mirror.

I ran my hands down my short black bob to smooth out the edges before I ran a comb straight down my blunt bangs. Today I chose to wear my new purple long-sleeved jumpsuit with the black belt and my new black wedge knee-high boots. The weather was turning to fall and it would be dark by the time I got home.

Mr. Prince Charming darted ahead of me. The smell of a fresh pot of coffee waited for me. Oscar was the best, making sure I had my cup of jolt before I headed out to work.

"As ready as I'll ever be," Madame Torres chimed in from her glass ball sitting on the kitchen counter. "I'm sort of sick of hearing about people's ailments." She cocked a brow; her purple eye shadow glistened. Her flaming red hair floated in the space around her. Her lips were painted a high red and her cheeks the same.

I opened the cabinet where I kept the mugs and grabbed my favorite one with the picture of a broom. It read: Don't Drink and Ride. Cracked me up every time I read it. I filled it up and took a few whiffs, letting the aroma wake up my senses before I took a drink. The most anticipated drink of the morning.

"Well? Are we going or not?" Madame Torres was good at ruining a moment.

"I was talking to Mr. Prince Charming, but I guess you should come along too." I took another long sip and looked outside the window above the kitchen sink.

It was a perfect view of all the shops in the village.

My cottage sits on the top of the hill behind the shops. I had a gorgeous view of the village and the backdrop of the mountains our town was nestled in. There was only one street in Whispering Falls, Main Street.

In the far distance on the right, Two Sisters and a Funeral was the first charming building to greet the visitors. It wasn't probably the best one since it was a funeral home, but it was gorgeous. The two-story Victorian was much different than the other shops in town, but it was also a much different type of business. The Karima sisters, Constance and Patience, owned and operated the funeral home. They were Ghost Whisper spiritualists and were good at their job. Though, they were always hoping to find a fresh dead body somewhere. You had to be careful if you ever closed your eyes, one of them would pick up your wrist to check for a pulse in a minute.

Down from Two Sisters was Wicked Good Bakery, owned and operated by Raven Mortimer along with the help of her sister Faith. Raven was an Aleuromancy spiritualist. Her visions came in the form of baking dough. Faith was a Clairaudience. She was able to hear things that were inaudible to the natural ear. It was cool when she would receive messages from the angels, guides, spirits or future.

Next to them was The Gathering Grove Tea Shoppe. Gerald Regiula, our only British citizen, was the master of fantastically brewed teas and coffee. He was a tealeaf reader. Next to his shop was Mystic Lights, the home of our crystal ball reader, Isadora Solstice. She had the latest and greatest, not to mention antique lighting elements that were popular and sought after from all over the world.

Ever After Books was next door to Izzy. Ophelia Biblio was the owner and operator of the beautiful bookshop. It was delightful to go in there and peruse the shelves. She was the typical witch in every sense of the word. What the mortals assumed to be a witch, Ophelia was that. Good one, though.

Across the street from Wicked Good was Bella's Baubles owned by village Astrologer Bella Van Lou. She has the most beautiful jewelry around. And Mr. Prince Charming was a frequent customer of hers.

Magical Moments, the florist in the village, was owned by Arabella Paxton, the daughter of Gerald. She made everything come to life. Her flowers and arrangements were all over Whispering Falls, adding life to the party.

Next to her was my shop. A Charming Cure. Then next to me was A Cleansing Spirit Spa where owner Chandra Shango looked into the future of her customers by reading their palms.

The last shop in the village, at the opposite end of Main Street from Two Sisters and A Funeral, was Glorybee Pet Shop. Petunia Shrubwood was the owner and animal spiritualist in the village. She recently married Gerald and tonight was a big night for her. She was going to take over as Village President. Currently, I held the presidency and had no intention of keeping it. I had a hard time staying neutral, taking in everyone's requests while keeping everyone else happy. I was gladly giving my short term over to her. Besides, she's been a spiritualist all her life. I've only been a spiritualist a short time.

On this cool crisp fall morning, the fog hung over the shops; it had a fascinating way of lifting just in time for the customers to stroll into town.

Mewl, mewl. Mr. Prince Charming jumped up on the counter, batting at me to hurry. He jumped back down.

Meow, meow. He darted between my legs, dragging his long white tail around my shins getting my jumper all hairy.

I bent down and picked him up, giving him a good scratch. "What would I ever do without you?" I snuggled him close.

He batted at my wrist.

"Yes." I had almost forgotten to wear my charm bracelet, which was something I knew I needed today.

The nightmare I had last night made my soul uneasy and my bracelet would keep me safe.

I put Mr. Prince Charming down and rushed back to my room, picking my charm bracelet up off the dresser. I dangled it in the air taking a good look at all the charms Mr. Prince Charming had given me over the years.

In fact it was my tenth birthday when he showed up on the doorstep of my house in Locust Grove. He was the cutest guy wearing a dingy collar with a silver turtle charm hanging off it.

Oscar and I had spent several days trying to find the owner and when no one came forward and Mr. Prince

Charming decided he was staying, Darla, my mom, let me keep him.

It wasn't until years later I had found out he was my fairy-god cat and brought me protection charms to keep me safe. Needless to say, I had several charms on my bracelet and if I ever needed protection, it was now. Especially since my nightmares had been returning.

I didn't have typical nightmares. When I had a nightmare, somehow they had a way of transpiring into the real world. *My* real world, hurting people I love.

"You have to stay close to me." I pointed a finger at Mr. Prince Charming.

Mewl.

"How do you stand being around the ball of fur?" Madame Torres curled her lip. She had never been a big fan of my cat. Well, she wasn't a big fan of anyone but herself.

"Whatever." I picked her up and stuck her in the bottom of my bag.

I would've left her at home, but having her with me made my uneasy stomach a little more at ease.

I grabbed my black long cloak off the hook next to the door, locked it behind me and headed out down the hill. It was a tad bit chilly and I needed a little more caffeine to chase the nightmare away.

Mr. Prince Charming darted in and out of the field of mums, his tail dancing above the golds, oranges, and browns dotting the hillside.

"Boo." Eloise Sandlewood snuck up behind me.

I nearly jumped out of my skin.

"Are you okay?" She peeled off the hood of her black cloak exposing her short red hair, a deep-set worry in her emerald eyes.

Eloise lived in a tree house a little beyond the wooded area behind my house. Of course I ran into her a lot, not only because we lived near one another, but she was also Oscar's aunt and Darla's best friend. She didn't own a shop, but she did cleanse the village every single night with her incense when everyone was gone and asleep.

"Oh honey." She grabbed me by the arms. "You aren't looking so good." She put her hand on my chin and moved my face side to side. "You know I love you like my own daughter. You have me worried." She grabbed my elbow and guided me down the hill toward town. "What is going on with you?"

It was true. Eloise was sort of my surrogate mother since my mother was deceased. She was Darla's confidant, her true friend. Darla hadn't been a spiritualist. She lived in the community for a short time while my dad, who was also deceased, was the police officer in Whispering Falls.

I guess what they say is true about a girl marrying a man like her father since Oscar was a lot like my dad.

"I'm having nightmares again." I confided in her more than I had Oscar. She would understand and I just needed a little girl talk. "Bad ones too."

"Do you have time for a coffee?" she asked, changing our course of path and heading us toward The Gathering Grove Tea Shoppe.

I glanced at my watch. I didn't have to open the shop for another half hour and I generally liked to go early to: make sure all the potions were filled, flip on my cauldron, and get ready for the day.

"I guess." I sucked in a deep breath. The nightmare still had me unnerved and maybe talking to Eloise would help out.

We hustled across the street and dipped into The Gathering Grove where Gerald Regiula was already helping a line full of customers. We tucked ourselves away at the corner café table by the window.

"Ladies," Gerald took his top hat off and tipped it toward us. "What do I owe the pleasure so early in the morning? Are you here because of the scuttlebutt of Full Moon?"

"Full moon?" Eloise asked. "It's definitely not a full moon."

"No, silly." Gerald scoffed. His mustache bounced up and down. "It's the new bed and breakfast in town. It went up like a firecracker. Overnight."

That was how things worked around here. Sometimes you wake up and there was a new business in town.

"The Elders must be busy." I sucked in a deep breath and wondered why there was a bed and breakfast opening up.

"Well, we are in need of a little pick-me-up jolt of caffeine." Eloise winked, untying the cloak from around her neck, changing the subject.

"A little pick-me-up you shall have." Gerald rubbed the edges of his mustache, his wedding ring bright and shiny.

"I must say, that ring looks mighty fine on you." I smiled, remembering the long journey to marriage he and Petunia had traveled down.

"Yes," his thick heavy English accent blurted out. "Love of my life."

"Oh, Daddy." Arabella Paxton walked up behind us with a large bouquet of fresh flowers in her arms. "I thought I was the love of your life." She winked, letting him off the hook and went about her way filling the empty flower vases on the tables with the fresh ones from her shop, Magical Moments.

I watched as Arabella's slim figure moved gracefully from table to table, creating the perfect designs on the spot. She was as lovely as her flowers. A rose herself with her long black flowing hair and crystal blue eyes to compliment her delicate features.

"I'll be back with a special just for you two." Gerald tented his fingertips and drummed them together in delight.

"We have to watch that one." Eloise lifted a brow.

There were rules to be a spiritualist and Gerald was notorious for trying to get around them. Rule Number One especially. It stated that a spiritualist cannot read another spiritualist unless given permission. Gerald had the gift of tealeaf reading, making it easy for him to read anyone in his shop.

"So, tell me what is going on?" she asked reaching over the table taking my hands in hers.

"I have been having new nightmares and they aren't good ones either." I tried to swallow the lump in my throat. The images of the nightmare tormented my memory. "It's about a fire. Me and Mr. Prince Charming are trapped in a building."

"What building?" she asked.

"I have no idea." I shook my head hoping to shake out some of the images of the dreams. "All I know is something in here," I pulled my hand out from underneath hers and pointed to my gut, "is telling me it isn't good. You know and I know, I'm right ninety-nine percent of the time."

"Do you think it's. . ." she paused, "Ezmeralda?"

"Stop," I said through gritted teeth. "Don't say her name. Don't." I ran my hand over my charm bracelet. I was going to need more than protective charms to deal with her. "Don't speak her name."

Ezmeralda was a beast from my past. Gerald's ex-wife and Arabella's mom who had turned to the Dark-Sider world of spirituality. She had vowed to come back to Whispering Falls to help me meet my demise. Something told me the nightmares had nothing to do with her. Or at least I hoped they didn't.

"I don't think it's her. My intuition isn't giving me that feeling." My intuition wasn't giving me any feeling but bad. That was why I had brought Madame Torres along with me.

She might be a snarky crystal ball, but she was my snarky crystal ball and had my best interest at heart. Maybe her best interest. Because if something happened to me, she didn't go anywhere but a garage sale or thrift store.

"Petunia is looking forward to the smudging ceremony tonight." Gerald set two cups of liquid in front of us, breaking the tension in the air between me and Eloise. "She is excited to have her family come in to see her become the Village President."

"Wonderful." I clapped my hands, trying to put the veiled threats from Ezmeralda behind me. "I'm excited for her."

Petunia had spent the last few months training with Isadora Solstice to become the next leader of our village. It was an honor given to me, but I was proven to be a little too young and not necessarily wanting to have the responsibility of the village on my shoulders. After all, my five-foot-four frame could barely hold all the issues I did have on my own. I was just fine being responsible for me, Mr. Prince Charming and Madame Torres with Oscar by my side. Tonight I would resign and give her the reins. Fine by me.

"This smells delicious. What is it?" Eloise asked, bringing the cup away from her nose.

"A special blend for cool fall mornings to put a spring in your step." He held his hand out and held his fingers up one-by-one. "1 Tbsp. fresh grated ginger, 2 cups filtered water, 1 Tbsp. raw honey or pure maple syrup, ½ lemon, juiced, 1 cinnamon stick, Chamomile flowers, from my daughter of course." A prideful smile appeared under his mustache. He continued, "Echinacea tincture, fresh mint leaves, pinch of cayenne pepper." He tapped his temple. "I think that is it."

"Did you leave the leaves out?" I swirled my cup in front of me looking into the liquid. He was known to put a few tea leaves in without the recipient knowing. And I didn't want anyone—other than who I told—to know about my dreams. It would send the town into a downward spiral.

"Of course I did." He shuffled off to help another table.

"Hm." I picked up my spoon and twirled it in the cup. There was a little skepticism in his tone. I lowered my eyes. "I wouldn't believe him even if I gave him a truth serum."

Eloise and I laughed.

"Does Oscar know about the nightmares?" She started back up the conversation I was ready to end.

"Unfortunately he saw how frantic I was when I woke up in the middle of the night." I recalled the look on his face. "But he doesn't know I've been having them nightly."

"He's spending the night?" Eloise drew back. She remained uncomfortably still.

Even though Oscar and I were spiritualists, Eloise still had old-fashioned ways. And spending the night before marriage was not appropriate. She made sure she was a parent to both of us.

"I'm glad he was there. I was so upset there was no way Madame Torres would have been able to comfort me. Or even sweet Mr. Prince Charming." I took a sip of the tea and set it back down on the saucer. "This is delicious."

"There you are." Oscar appeared behind me. He bent down and kissed my forehead. "I went to the shop but your sign was still turned to closed."

He walked around and gave his aunt a kiss before he put a small paper sack on the table and I knew what was in it before he even told me.

"I thought you could use a little treat." He smiled and pushed the Wicked Good Bakery bag toward me. "And Raven said it just came out of the oven."

"You are so sweet." Eloise grinned. "I can't wait to see what your babies are going to look like."

"Hello?" My eyes widened. I was just getting used to the idea I was engaged; not even close on having children. "Cart before the horse."

"No joking." Oscar looked so handsome in his Whispering Falls police uniform. "I've got to get going.

Colton said we are expecting a crowd for Petunia's ceremony tonight. I also kind of told him we would grab a bite to eat with him and Ophelia beforehand."

"That's good." The more distractions the better.

"Take care of each other." He kissed Eloise and me again. "You are the most important girls in my life." He bent down again. He whispered in my ear, "You are the most important." His mouth moved over mine with exquisite tenderness replacing the knot in my stomach with a tingling.

Eloise and I sat in silence watching Oscar leave and walk down the sidewalk toward the station.

"You two are so adorable. I just can't stand it." Eloise picked up her cup and took a sip. "But we need to figure out these dreams."

"I've even used my mom's fairy dust potion and it's not working." My mom was a homeopathic curist; she just wasn't able to make potions and get to the root of someone's aliment since she wasn't a spiritualist.

She left me a secret book of spells (Magical Cures Book) she had gotten from Eloise, and I had scoured it to find some sort of new potion to help me get rid of these terrible nightmares.

"Fire nightmares aren't anything to mess around with." Eloise wasn't making me feel any better.

"Tell me about it." I drank the last sip of tea from the cup and got up. I didn't leave without the bag from Wicked Good Bakery. It would be a treat for later. "I've got to get going. I have to find out where Mr. Prince Charming went before I open the shop. I have to keep him close."

"I'll be by later to check on you." Eloise nodded. "I'm going to have another cup of this delicious brew." She lifted her hand in the air. Gerald acknowledged another round with a big grin. I waved 'bye and headed out the door.

"June! June!" Petunia waved her hands in the air. With each bobble of her head, a butterfly flew out from her messy updo, knocking out a few twigs as well.

A few people trailed behind her. She held a bag from Wicked Good in her hand. "We just came from the bakery and I told my family the June's Gems were to die for. Especially since they were named after one of my friends."

That was one of Petunia's personality traits I loved. She thought everyone was her best friend. And everyone did love her. She had a sunny disposition and her love of all creatures exuded from her.

"They are delicious." I held the bag in the air. "I'm saving mine for an afternoon treat."

June's Gems was Raven Mortimer's take on a Ding Dong. The chocolaty treat was my favorite. We had seen a lot of stressful times together. The Ding Dong knew how to calm me down. Since we didn't have a supply of Ding Dongs in Whispering Falls, Raven was gracious enough to make an even better version, naming it after me.

True or not (I like to lean toward the true side), Raven said June's Gem was her best seller.

"This is my sister, Peony." She pointed to the girl next to her, who looked very young. The light blue wrap dress made her blue eyes pop against her pale skin tone. Her small hands gave a slight wave hello before she ran her hand down her high blond ponytail. I couldn't help but feel a little envious of her taupe stilettos. Definitely got the fashion sense of the two sisters.

"Nice to meet you." I nodded, offering a smile.

"My cousin, Gwendolyn." Petunia showcased her cousin like she was on display, just like one of those game shows on television. "Gwenie for short. But she's just like a sister to us." Petunia looked at Peony giving a quick nod. Peony backed her up.

Gwendolyn was a little plumper than the other two. Her hair was not as messy as Petunia's and not as neat as Peony. She was a mix between the two of them. Her hair was brown like Petunia's and pulled into a bun. She folded her arms in front of her. Her dark eyes lowered. There was not a smile on her face as there was Petunia's and Peony's.

We politely nodded, neither of us smiling.

Petunia's arms curled around the third woman. "This is my bestest friend in the entire world. Amethyst Plum. They are here for my induction. But Amethyst is here forever."

"So nice to meet you." I shook each of their hands, not getting a good feeling from cousin Gwendolyn. "Forever?"

"Yes." Amethyst said with a flat voice. She wore a black pair of pants and a black buttoned blouse. Her black hair lay in loose curls down her back. Her thick black brows arched perfectly over her dark eyes. Her long lashes swooped down with each blink. She was beautiful. The only pop of color was the tips of her red heels. "I own Full Moon."

Petunia clasped her hands in front of her, twirling her body from side-to-side, grinning from ear-to-ear.

"June owns A Charming Cure, with all sorts of homeopathic cures." Petunia nodded enthusiastically. "You will get to know each other really well. And," Petunia squealed. "You can join our book club! We meet once a month at Ever After Books. You are going to love it."

"We will see." Amethyst's brows rose.

"Really? You own A Charming Cure?" Peony bounced on her toes. She grabbed Amethyst. "Isn't that cool?"

"No." Gwenie quipped. "I go to a doctor. A real doctor." Her eyes lowered, glaring at me. "Aren't you the one who took the Village President's job right out from underneath my cousin?"

"I..." I stuttered. "I didn't. . ."

"Gwenie!" Petunia's hand clasped over her mouth. "That's in the past."

"She's just asking a question," Amethyst chirped in. "I'd like to hear the answer."

Gwenie never took her eyes off me, making me a bit uncomfortable. "Aren't you?" She wasn't going to let it die.

"June, I'm sorry for their behavior." Petunia stepped up and nervously fiddled with a strand of stray hair that had fallen out of her updo. "Gwenie's just looking out for me. I'm sure Amethyst is nervous about Full Moon opening. It's her first shop. After all. . ."

Amethyst's voice was bold. "You did call me every day for a month complaining about her and how she stole it right out from underneath you after you had been working toward it all your life."

"But that was before I knew the chosen one was among our village," Petunia said.

She was right. I had no idea why or how I was the chosen one, but I was. Evidently I wasn't the chosen one to be the Village President because I just couldn't do it. In my gut, there was a task out there for me as the chosen one, only I hadn't found out what the task was. I figured it would rear its ugly head. In the meantime, I couldn't worry about the task and had to live my life.

"Don't sugar coat it." Peony laughed elbowing Amethyst. "Really she means no harm."

"I think you are way off base." I wasn't going to stand there and let her accuse me of coming to Whispering Falls to deliberately take the Village President dream from Petunia. "You have no idea what you are talking about and until you do. . ."

"What?" Amethyst questioned me.

"Oh dear." Petunia wrung her hands. "Oh dear."

"Yeah, what?" Gwenie took a step forward.

"What potion girl? Are you going to give me some evil potion to shut me up?" Amethyst stood tall and scared me a little. She tapped the toe of her shoe.

Cousin Gwendolyn took another step closer like they were some gang backing each other up. "Because I'm here to tell you no one, not even a little two-bit potion witch is going to hurt my family."

"Is something going on here?" Colton Lance stepped up behind us.

Colton took his police hat off; his messy blond hair fell down around his ears. He and Ophelia were an item. They came to Whispering Falls together and they lived above Ever After Books. He was in charge of the police department after a misunderstanding with Oscar a few months back, but now they were both in charge.

"Colton." Petunia's worry lines softened. "This is my sister, Peony, my best friend, Amethyst, and my cousin, Gwendolyn."

Colton was gracious enough to shake their hands before he turned to me. "Are you okay, June?"

Gwendolyn and Amethyst walked off toward Glorybee.

"I'm fine. Just looking for that ornery cat of mine," I looked past Colton to make sure they weren't going to A Charming Cure's line of customers.

"Oh cute white one?" Petunia's sister asked bringing me back to the present conversation. Petunia's face balled with a smile and her head nodded. "He was at Glorybee."

"Yes. I would guess that." The fog was slowly lifting and some cars were driving by. I had to get the shop open.

"He's a little charmer that one." Peony smiled.

"Yes, he is. He loves a pretty face." I instantly liked Peony. Anyone who loved my cat, I liked. He didn't just like anyone either.

"We might have given him a few treats before we walked down here." Petunia blushed knowing I had asked her to stop giving him so many since he was putting on a little weight.

"I better get going," I said before I started to cross the street. There was a line already forming outside of A Charming Cure.

"I love the name of your shop." Peony and Petunia crossed with me.

"Thank you. I'm a little partial to it." I could feel the pride written on my face. I knew Petunia had already told her, but maybe she was so young she had forgotten. She seemed a little flighty.

The shop has come a far way since my days of selling the homeopathic cures in the Locust Grove Flea Market.

"Can we go in there later?" She turned to Petunia.

"Of course." Petunia bent down and picked up a fallen tree branch off the road and stuck it in her hair. "I want to take you into every shop before you go back home."

"See you soon." I waved and darted between the cars like a human game of Frogger. Colton had crossed

the sidewalk a distance down and he seemed to be
waiting on me.

"Was Petunia's friend threatening you?" Colton
asked when I approached him.

"No." I shook my head refusing to let her ruin
Petunia's moment. "I'm sure she's nervous about Full
Moon."

"It sure sounded like she threatened you and you
said something about casting a spell on her." His words
stopped me dead in my tracks.

"I did no such thing." I had to clarify. "She badgered
me." My words came out more frantic than I wanted
them too.

"So she did threaten you?" he asked again.

"She was only taking up for her best friend," I
assured him. "Something about the history between me
and Petunia with the whole Village President thing. But
that is going to be corrected tonight."

"You said she badgered you." He cocked a brow.

"She asked if I was going to put some sort of spell on
her or something because I started to take up for myself

before I decided to let it go." I tucked a piece of hair under my chin. His questions were making me nervous. "Ridiculous."

"What did you say about a shop?" Colton asked.

"Amethyst owns the new bed and breakfast in town." I looked around to see where it was. "Full Moon."

"So, that's her." Colton's head went from side-to-side, trying to get a look at Petunia and the girls off in the distance. "I heard there was a new shop, but it's on the outskirts of town. Something about the Elders not wanting visitors to see all the magical happenings in the middle of the night."

"I never thought of it, but I guess it makes sense." I shrugged. "I'm just a bit shocked they approved a sleepover shop. I never thought we'd need a bed and breakfast. The Elders must be busy."

The Order of Elders consisted of three past Village Presidents from different villages. They approved shops for all the villages and came when there was a crime committed. I had gotten to know them pretty well when I had found myself a suspect in a crime I had not committed. The Marys, as I so lovingly called them since their names were Mary Sue, Mary Ellen and Mary Lynn, were harmless.

I had a sneaky suspicion I was going to see them while they were in town. I scoffed the idea away and took off toward my shop.

Chapter Three

I opened the beautiful gate in front of the store; every store had the most amazing gates and doors welcoming the customers inside to a world of magic.

Two little window boxes under each window had fresh flowers. It didn't take a potion to know Arabella had replaced my dead ones. Fortunately the outside of the shop was covered in the most beautiful wisteria vine, which didn't require much maintenance. Good for me since I would surely have killed it.

The purple and white flowers grew up and around the front door. It was a welcoming sight each morning. Especially on cold foggy mornings like today. Instant happiness, I thought smiling as I looked at the vine.

"Outta the way. Excuse me." I heard someone behind me when I stuck the key into the shop door. "Move it."

I turned around to see the line of customers being shoved to the right and left as Patience and Constance Karima made their way to the front.

They two grey-haired sisters who owned Two Sisters and a Funeral, pushed their way to the front. They were always on the look out for fresh bodies. They didn't care who was in their way. When they wanted something they took it. Patience, the shorter of the two, stood behind Constance.

"Yes," Patience was the master of repeating her sister. "Outta the way."

"Constance. Patience." I tilted my head to the side. I blew my bangs out of my face. "It's not very nice to cut line in front of these nice people."

I had to make good somehow. There were some angry faces in the crowd.

"We must wait our turn." I smiled and turned the key to open the door, trying to hurry in without them following me.

Constance must not have heard me, or she ignored me because she plowed on through the door even before I could make it in. The bell above the door rapidly swung back and forth, dinging in our ears.

"Welcome," I said flatly. "I guess you aren't waiting your turn," I muttered under my breath. I could tell it was going to be one of *those* days.

I flipped on the light switch next to the door and greeted each customer who came in. "Calming the soul products are on the left and anything pertaining to health issues are on the right. You will find wonderful products in the middle for facials and other external healings you might need."

"We didn't come here for no cleansing," Constance protested. Her jaws clenched, her cheek muscles stood out.

"No cleansing," Patience repeated, wringing her hands together. "Someone's gonna die."

A couple customers' heads turned.

"Oh, I do have some embalming fluid for you." I grabbed each of them and pulled them to the back of the shop not letting go until we were out of hearing range. "What is wrong with you two?"

"Oh stop it." Constance smacked my hand away. Patience followed. "You aren't the Village President anymore. I'm telling you. Something evil is lurking. It's the evil feeling I get when someone is about to eeck." She dragged her stubby fat finger across her neck.

Patience mimicked her. "Eeck."

I put my bag on the counter and flipped the switch on my cauldron that was hiding from the world to see behind the small partition next to the counter. I wanted to protest and assure them nothing of the sort was going to happen but the glow from the bottom of my purse confirmed Madame Torres was trying to tell me something.

"I will look into it," was the only assurance I could give them.

Neither of them had satisfied looks on their faces from my answer, but it was all I had. Constance turned and huffed away, Patience puffed along behind her. With a smile on my face, I greeted each customer we passed as I walked them to the door.

"Are you dying?" Patience asked a woman looking at the facial creams.

"I'm sorry," I apologized to the customer, whose face had paled. "She's leaving."

I opened the door and pushed the sisters out onto the steps. Mr. Prince Charming darted in. I closed the door and peeled the curtain back on the window, watching the sisters stop everyone in their path, talking to them.

They were probably scaring the daylights out of the tourists. I couldn't worry with them. I had customers and nightmares to deal with.

"Excuse me." A young woman with a small child wrapped around her leg had a bottle of Monsters Be Gone, a homeopathic cure for children who won't go to sleep because they are afraid of monsters under the bed. "I was wondering how I use this?"

"Oh," I held my hand out and she gave me the bottle.

My intuition got nothing from her but some anxious feeling. I gently reached down and touched the child on the head. Instantly my intuition went on high alert. Not only was the child afraid of monsters, the women in the neighborhood were gossiping about the child, discouraging their children from playing with him.

"I've got just what you need." I held my finger in the air. "If you will wait right here, I will go put in the extra ingredients."

I walked back to the counter and behind the partition where my cauldron was ready to go. I uncorked the bottle of Monsters Be Gone and poured the liquid into the pot. I ran my finger along the shelf behind me that was lined with bottles of special ingredients. The Slippery Elm ingredient glowed to my touch, letting me know it was the perfect herb to use and add to the Monsters Be Gone to halt the gossip.

"Ah, Passion Flowers." My insides grinned when the bottle lit up.

Passion Flowers was one of my favorite ingredients. It promoted a lot of things such as peacefulness, sleep, and friendship. Something the little child could use a lot of. I turned back to the cauldron where the liquid was starting to bubble.

The bubbling, murky, thin fluid was rose in color. I used the ladle to slowly stir to a simmer before adding a dash of Slippery Elm. Instantly the fluid bubbled to the top smelling like mud. I put my finger in and took a quick taste.

"Um." It might smell like muddy little boys, but it tasted like rich creamy chocolate.

That was how my potions worked. The child might be scared of monsters, but the bigger problem was the gossiping around it, the bullying from the others. The potions really made themselves and the taste was automatically what the child liked best. It smelled like mud because he loved to play in the mud or be outside. Either way, this was his special homeopathic cure and once they tried it, it would work. He would have tons of friends and no longer be scared of monsters, leaving me with a satisfied customer who would return for more cures. That was how this town was so special.

The swirling liquid was now a deep sapphire blue. The pinch of Passion Flower sprinkled in sent little bursts of fireworks above the pot. My insides were smiling, but my soul still ached from the nightmare I had last night and I knew I was going to have to deal with it sooner or later.

I let the mixture come to a boil while I picked out the perfect bottle. I turned back to the shelf and once again ran my finger along the empty glass containers. Like always, when I got to the one meant for this little boy and his special cure, it lit up.

The bottle made me pause, wondering if I had gotten it wrong. But it glowed green, pulsing like it had a heartbeat. The skull on the front made me a little leery, but I went with it and took it off the shelf.

With the ladle, I scooped out the liquid and poured it into the brown bottle with the skull on the front. Once it was filled to the top, I put the cork top on and pushed down to make sure it was nice and snug.

"Here you go." I walked up to the mom and son.

When he saw the bottle, his eyes—so clouded when he walked in the shop—cleared.

"I love it. Can I eat some now?" He grabbed the bottle out of my hands.

"We don't grab from people," his mom scolded him. She bent down to his level. "The nice lady will tell us how to use it, honey." The mom stood up and thanked me, apologizing once more for the child grabbing the bottle out of my hands.

"It's not a problem. It is his, just like he knows it is." I smiled at the child. He held the bottle in his hands and then grabbed my leg.

"Thank you, Doctor Lady." The boy grinned from ear to ear. There was already a shift in him before he had even taken the first dose.

"Now, just use a little at night by rubbing it on his face and neck like a cream." I rubbed my hands together and then along my neck to show them how to apply.

"It's not digestible?" The mom looked confused.

"Oh no." I looked down at the boy. "The directions are also printed on the label."

"Can I use it now?" The boy asked without even waiting for the answer. He had the bottle unscrewed and was wiping it down his neck and all over his cheeks.

"Umm. . ." Nighttime or now, but nighttime would've been better, but I kept my mouth shut and a smile planted on my face.

"I guess we have to pay you now." There was a grateful look on the mom's face. "He hasn't been this confident in weeks. Thank you."

"You are so welcome. I'm happy to help." I took her money. "If you have any more issues, which I don't think you will, please feel free to come back."

"Oh, I will be back." The mom gathered the little boy and headed out the door.

Meow, meow. Mr. Prince Charming sat on the counter and watched them leave.

"Another satisfied customer." I ran my hand down my wonderful fairy-god cat and turned my attention from the shop door to him.

There was never a happier feeling than using my spiritual gift to help someone. Then the shift from elation to apprehension hit me like a ton of bricks when I saw the triangle-shaped charm lying between Mr. Prince Charming's front two paws.

Chapter Four

"Faith," I gasped above the crowded shop when I saw my blond-haired friend walk in. "I'm so glad to see you."

"I thought you were going to say that." She smiled, meandering her way through the customers and back to me. "I had a feeling I needed to come in and help out." She glanced around the hopping shop. "And by the looks of things, I was spot on. You could use an extra hand around here."

"Yes, I could." I held the charm in between my finger and thumb. With my free hand I got my cape. "But right now I have to get down to Bella's Baubles and need you to man the shop."

"Sure." She shrugged. "I love it here. Go on."

Everyone helped everyone around Whispering Falls. Faith was a Clairaudience. She was able to hear things that were inaudible to the common ear. Spirit guides, angels, and hearing into the future were her specialty. I

believed my spirit guide was my mother Darla. I had only
seen her once in the great beyond, but knew I would see
her more as I became more and more familiar with my
spiritual world.

"Excuse me." I nearly knocked over a customer on
their way in and my way out. I threw my cape around my
shoulders. Cold crisp air danced around my ankles. The
fall weather was coming. "Peony. Amethyst." I was
shocked to see Petunia's sister and friend, especially
Amethyst. Didn't she have a shop to take care of?

"We wanted to stop in your shop and see what you
have before I leave tomorrow." Peony said. She was so
very different than Petunia.

"But it looks like you were on your way out and
fast." Amethyst faced me but her eyes were shifting
around the shop. "We can come back later."

"But I wanted to find out about the ceremony for
tonight and see if you needed anything." Peony
generously offered. "Besides, when is later? We have the
ceremony tonight and tomorrow I'm leaving. You get to
stay here. Not me." Peony huffed like a child.

"I'm going back to Full Moon." Amethyst shoved past us and dashed down the steps. "You can do what you want. You are a grown woman."

"She's so nervous about Full Moon not being fully occupied with the ceremony and all." Peony's lips went into a thin line. She said, "I told her not to be a Debbie downer because everyone here would know it with our spiritual gifts and all."

My palm tightened around the triangle charm. I wish I had gotten a good look at it because I was dying to get down to Bella to see what it was protection over, but I didn't want to be rude to Peony.

"I'm not sure about other villages, but in Whispering Falls, you aren't allowed to read any other spiritualist unless they approve it. It's a law. So you don't to have to worry about being read here. I guess I should say something to Amethyst." I shrugged. I held my clinched fist in the air. "I've got to get going though. If you want to come back an hour before the ceremony, I'd love to have you help me get ready for your sister's big night."

"Really?" Her eyes shot open. The sudden element of surprise rose on her face.

"Sure." I laughed.

I never had a sibling. It must've made Petunia feel good her family and friends were so supportive and willing to be here. After all, it wasn't every day your sister became a Village President. It was a pretty big deal. Petunia was up for it. She'd been training for it for a long time. She had studied every possible gift there was and was liked by many. Including me.

"Hi, Arabella." Peony must've been satisfied with my answer. She headed next door to Magical Moments.

"Thanks for the window box flowers," I said to Arabella and pointed to the arrangements.

"No problem." Arabella waved before she and Peony ducked into the flower shop.

I shook my head. Peony and Petunia were alike in the friend department. Neither of them seemed to know a stranger. Peony hadn't been in town a few hours and she already knew everyone by name.

Bella's Baubles was like all the other stores in Whispering Falls. A quaint cream cottage with a pink wood door was adorned with different colored jewels. The sun had burnt off the cold fall chill, and hit each jewel just right, showing its brilliant color.

Bella was my landlord of the cute cottage until I found out my parents had owned it and it really belonged to me. Bella and I were good friends. When I first moved to Whispering Falls, she took the time to get me acquainted with who owned what and the entire scoop on the village. I could count on her for many things.

Her store hours read *Mornin' to Night* and it cracked me up every time I read it.

Ding, ding. The bell above the door swayed back and forth when I opened it.

"I wondered when you were going to be here." Bella looked up. Her long blond hair cascaded down the front of her.

I was used to seeing the gap between her two front teeth and balled up cheeks from her smile when I came in, but not today. She remained uncomfortably still, making me panic a little bit.

"I was a little taken aback when Mr. Prince Charming showed up this morning and picked out the third eye charm." She took the loupe away from her eye and stood up from the wheelie chair she used to move around the glass counter from customer to customer.

Her smoky eyes held my gaze when her five-foot-two frame walked around to greet me. She took her hand and placed it over mine. I opened it and let the charm fall into hers.

"In the center of the triangle is the eye we call the third eye." She held it up for me to see. "You need to keep your eyes open at all times. You feel the evil in the air. The nightmares have returned and you aren't getting much sleep. You need to let Mr. Prince Charming and Madame Torres do their jobs at night while you get your rest."

I tried to take in all she was saying and listened for a positive spin on it, only there wasn't any sort of happy on her face or in her voice.

"Do you understand what I'm saying?" Bella was an Astrologer. She was the expert on charts and gems.

"Unfortunately, I do think I do." I sucked in a deep breath and watched her unclasp my charm bracelet off my wrist. "One problem, I can't get my rest when I suddenly wake up from these nightmares."

"You are going to have to force yourself out of the nightmare before it's too late." Her words sent chills up my spine. I grabbed the edges of my cloak and tugged it around my neck.

Bella returned to her post behind the counter.

"I see Petunia's family has started to trickle in," Bella's voice turned chipper—much different than a few seconds ago. She grabbed a few tools and laid my bracelet out on a black cloth in front of her. She sat down in her chair and put her eye loupe back in her eye. "I'm excited to see what their spiritual gifts are. Especially her friend Amethyst since she's now one of us."

"Yeah." I was too preoccupied with the danger lurking and wondered if Eloise was right and it was Ezmeralda making good on her promise to me.

"Listen," Bella's chin was tucked under as she worked on getting the charm on my bracelet. "Don't let this hinder you from living. You never know. Wearing the charm might ward off the evil spirit and maybe nothing will happen. Believe in Mr. Prince Charming. Believe in Madame Torres. They are your familiars to protect you."

"I do believe in them, but how much do I tell Oscar?" I asked. "He has so much on his plate. He's trying to work as the sheriff and going to Wizardly School at Hidden Halls. It might be too much for him to take on." I wasn't sure what to do. "I didn't even tell him about my nightmares. Then he spent the night and I had one right in front of him."

"Oh," The gap between her teeth I had longed to see appeared along with her balled-up cheeks and a big sympathy grin across her small face. "You two have really stepped things up. Sleepover and all."

"I couldn't imagine my life without him." A warm fuzzy feeling settled in my heart, making the chill on my spine warm. I peeled off the cloak and laid it in my lap.

I couldn't wait for Oscar to get off work so I could let him know what was going on. It was the right thing to do.

"Luckily you don't have to." She dangled my bracelet in the air. The third eye staring right at me.

Chapter Five

I had taken a little longer than I wanted to with Bella. Time felt like it stood still when I was with her. The cold wind hit me as soon as I stepped out of Bella's Baubles. I swung my cloak and wrapped it around my shoulders. I ducked my head away from the chilly wind, and made my way down the sidewalk to A Charming Cure, making a quick detour behind the shops.

"Don't fail me now." I held my hands out to the side. The sleeves of my cape dangled along with my charm bracelet. I sucked in a deep breath with my eyes closed. When I felt the next cold breeze blow my blunt bangs away from my face, I whispered into the wind, "Universe, Spirits, Angels and Guides. Receive my eternal gratitude for all that is. I ask for clearer guidance, as I will listen with a sharper ear. May this talisman heighten my intuition. To receive your messages more clearly. So mote it be."

The branches howled as though the Universe was talking back to me, receiving my prayer, my desires and my needs.

I knew I should get back to the shop and let Faith go back to her job, but I couldn't stop my mouth from chanting. My fists balled, I opened my fingers wide, my fists balled again, pumping blood through my veins. It was important as ever to hear my intuition.

A tree branch snapped, popping my eyes open. Through a clearing behind Glorybee, I saw a couple women walking and talking.

"I'm thrilled they have the new bed and breakfast, Maple," the one said to the other.

"Me too. Now we can take our time through the shops and not rush around in one day." The two scurried off toward town.

"That way," I sighed and headed in the direction from where they had emerged. "Yep. That way." I smiled as Mr. Prince Charming darted out from behind a tree and down the path leading me to the front steps of Full Moon Bed and Breakfast Treesort. Faith was going to have to hold down the fort at the shop a little longer. Not only was my intuition telling me to check out Full Moon, my curiosity was with my cat and I was going to chase him.

"What in the hell?" My eyes squinted trying to take in the massive structure nestled deep within in the forest among other trees.

"It's a Treesort." Amethyst caught me off guard. A smile upon her face. "I knew there was nothing like it around here, except Eloise Sandlewood's home. They are very popular in the villages out west, but I'm assuming you know that since you were the Village President."

Ahem, I cleared my throat. I wasn't sure I wanted to fight or run. I decided to fight when I saw Mr. Prince Charming dart up the stairs.

"I think you have my history all wrong." I started to say but she rudely interrupted me.

"Since your familiar has decided to take a tour, would you like to follow?" she asked, talking about Mr. Prince Charming.

"Yes. I'd love to." The fight was not in me. Keeping the peace was. "This is a very interesting concept."

I had to admit, I was intrigued. I followed her up the double-decker set of steps to the A-frame wooden structure, seeing nothing but a wall full of windows.

The inside of the resort reminded me of the interior of a ski lodge. In the middle of the open large room, a stone fireplace warmed the room with the roaring fire. All the walls were floor to ceiling windows giving the most spectacular views of Whispering Falls.

"Here is where our customers can come and get a snack and on the other side of the fireplace is the large kitchen. The breakfast side of the business." Amethyst's heels clicked, her skirt swooshed around the fireplace.

The other side had two large farm tables and benches on each side. They were set with dishes, utensils, chalices, and cloth napkins ready for someone to sit and partake in the delicious smells coming from the boiling pot on the gas stove.

"I'm making beef stew if you would like to sample." Amethyst slid with grace over to the stove and slowly stirred the soul-warming food.

"I'm good." I patted my stomach. "But this is amazing."

"When I approached the Elders about my idea, they loved it." She tented the pads of her fingers and drummed them. "I told them I was going to visit my friend in Whispering Falls and they told me there was a desperate need for something exactly like this due to the rapid economic growth of the community."

"Yes." I shook my head and grabbed Mr. Prince Charming off the counter next to the stove. He definitely wanted a taste of the stew. I held him in my arms and stroked him. "I'm shocked it's in the forest. Great concept, but forest?"

"Where else can you have a Treesort?" Amethyst chuckled in a condescending way. "I mean, it adds to our, let's say, magical feel of the community."

"Oh, it does," I agreed, but something tugged at my intuition. I swallowed the lump and rubbed my bracelet letting the emotion float away. "I can't believe how beautiful it is up here."

I walked over to the windows, taking in the views. The mountains still had fog sitting around the tops of them, barely making them visible. When the fog lifted, it had to be the most amazing view.

"Over there is one of the cabins." Amethyst pointed to another tree house in a tree in the distance.

"What?" I was confused.

"Full Moon is a Treesort. This is the main building but the guests sleep and shower in their own tree house." She pointed around to different trees. Suddenly they all came into focus. "The sunsets are beautiful from any room and the moon is always full." She grinned. "You really should come back tonight after your little smudging ceremony because I'm having a celebration party for Petunia."

Maybe my little trip out here was just what Amethyst and I needed to call a truce to whatever tension was between us.

"That's nice of you." I smiled and glanced back out the window. "Can we take a look at one of the guest rooms?"

"Sure." She motioned for me to follow her.

I put Mr. Prince Charming down and he followed right along, down the steps. With our feet on solid ground, we hurried east where not too far off in the distance was a round tree house. The path between each tree house was marvelous. Tiny white lights dangled along the tree branches lighting the way. Pops of colorful flowers dotted the path.

"Singing Nettles." I stopped when I heard the hum of the flower my mother loved so dearly.

"Yes. They are hidden among the ferns. As they are magic and could throw off any mortal." Her finger pointed to them as they happily swayed and hummed. "Here we are. My only opening tonight. I do wish I was sold out though."

"You will once the tourists hear about it." There was no way she wouldn't be. It was a fascinating concept for a hotel and anyone who loved Whispering Falls, would love this. "I'd be more than happy to put Full Moon brochures on my counter."

The way I saw it, if Full Moon was thriving, so was the rest of the village. Win, win.

The steps up to the round tree house looked as if they were floating.

"If you don't mind me asking, what is your spiritual gift?" I asked as curiosity stung my gut.

"Oneircritic." She waved her hands in the air. "I interpret dreams. So this little adventure is perfect in a town that seems to suit my needs and I get to be with Petunia."

Dream interpreter?

I bit back the idea swirling in my head about telling her about my dreams. It wasn't like I could trust her. We weren't fast friends and we really didn't have any history that didn't have tension around it. Not to mention my gut still tugged at me, along with my dream.

I ran my hand over my wrist, feeling for the third eye charm. Mr. Prince Charming darted up the floating steps like it was no big deal along with Amethyst. I took my time, a bit scared of how sturdy they were.

"Tell me, June," Amethyst stopped at the top. Her skirt swooshed as she abruptly stopped. "Do you have dreams? Or *nightmares*?"

I grabbed the side rails of the floating stairs as they swayed back and forth. A burst of wind came out of nowhere, sending what leaves were left on the autumn trees tumbling. The wind picked up again, the leaves swirled in tornado form around my feet, moving up and around my body.

Amethyst clapped her hands. The wind died.

"I. . ." I wasn't sure what to say. It wasn't as though I trusted Amethyst to know what was going on, nor were we friends. Plus I wasn't sure what had just happened with the wind and the leaves. My breath quickened. My pulse pounded. I let go of the rail and grabbed my wrist.

"I mean, if you ever need anyone to talk to about your dreams, I'm here and waiting." She turned back around and continued as if nothing had just happened. "Every guest house has a bedroom or two, depending on the size rented, along with a bathroom and a small refrigerator. Plus an amazing balcony." She stood at the top of the steps with her back to me and her gaze crossed in front of her. "I was very happy with the outcome. The Order of Elders were very accommodating."

"Wow." My jaw dropped. "Spectacular."

"There isn't a bad view from any of the ten tree house options." Amethyst opened the door and let us in.

The little house was decorated very romantically. A large fluffy couch and chairs along with fancy French chic furniture. The bedroom was just as fancy with the off-white décor and the four-poster King bed was draped in sheer curtains and dangling lights.

"A good night's sleep is guaranteed here." Her eyes lit when she smiled. She whispered, "Magic."

Meowl, meowl, hiss. Mr. Prince Charming darted out the door and down the steps.

Amethyst straightened tall and stuck her chin in the air. Her eyes lowered.

"I guess that is my clue to leave. I've overextended myself. Mr. Prince Charming is good at letting me know." I felt I needed to make excuses for his sudden ill behavior, but the words of Bella sang in my memory. *Listen to Mr. Prince Charming.*

"Yes." She stood on the balcony. "I'm sure you can find your way back to town."

"Thank you for showing me around. It's truly lovely." Slowly I walked down the steps and didn't look back. If I did, I knew her stare would run through my veins.

Maybe my little visit didn't do anything for the tension.

Chapter Six

I was pleasantly surprised to see A Charming Cure's shelves were practically empty. Faith had sold almost all the premade potions. She was such a natural at sales.

"You have been busy." I smiled on the outside, but inwardly groaned when I saw how much I was going to have to make in the late hours of the night. The ceremony for me to resign as Village President and hand it over to Petunia would go well into the night. There was no way I would have time in the morning to get all the potions made.

Still, I wasn't complaining. It was a good day. All I had to do was up my production to double what I thought I needed. Plus I could store them in the little room off the back where I kept a refrigerator and a couch for late nights such as the one I was going to have tonight.

"You have been gone a while." Faith pointed to the clock on the wall. "You have so many repeat customers." She pointed over to one long-time customer, Adeline.

"Adeline!" I was delighted to see her.

She was my link to the outside world I grew up in. She was the owner of the Piggly Wiggly in Locust Grove, Kentucky, my hometown where I'd lived with Darla. Oscar had lived across the street. In fact, his first job was with the Locust Grove Police. This was all before we knew we were spiritualists.

His parents were also spiritualists, making him a wizard. He was much better with a gun than a wand. Either way he was devilishly handsome.

"You look great." I put my arms around her. She gave me a quick hug.

"You look a little tired." She took a good look at me before she jumped up and squealed. "Oh my God! Is that what I think it is?"

She pulled my hand up to her face. Her jaw dropped. My mom's diamond sparkled. I couldn't stop myself from smiling. I felt like a schoolgirl.

"You and Mr. Hotty?" She referred to Oscar.

I didn't have to answer. The smile on my face said more than words ever could.

"Wow! I've not been here in awhile, but last time I was, Oscar was dating someone else." She reminded me of unhappier times.

"Things change." My shoulders lifted. "Say, what's going on with you?"

"Not much. I wanted to stop by on my day off and get some refills." She had a litany of bottles in her hands. She loved getting the facial creams.

"Sorry to bug you, but I've got to get going." Faith said her goodbyes and passed Peony on the way out.

She was dressed to the nines. Her hair was long and straight. Her eyes were lined with black liner, her lips candy-apple red, and she wore a long-sleeved tight, black knit dress you would see a mortal wear on Halloween.

"I can't wait to see what potions you make for Petunia's ceremony." Peony clapped her hands.

She was definitely the younger of the two.

"Excuse us for just a minute," I said to Peony and took Adeline by the arm, dragging her clear across the room.

"What was that about with Elvira?" Adeline nervously laughed.

"We get all kinds in here." I smiled trying to cover up Peony's immature mistake. "You look great."

"Thanks. It's all the yoga." She put her hands in prayer pose and nodded her head slightly forward. "Which you should come to one night."

"I just might take you up on that offer." I ran my hands down her arm, my intuition picking up on nothing, which was good. "Do you still live in the same house?"

"Yep." She rocked back on her heels. "Anyway, what do I owe you for all this?"

"Nothing." I waved her off and watched the last bit of customers leave for the day. "You are my friend. I will refill your soul anytime."

"You know." She cocked her head. "That is exactly what you do. You fill my soul." She smirked. "And to think I'm trying to get you to come back to Locust Grove and do yoga." She shook her head and walked to the door. I opened it for her. "Seriously, come by and see me. I miss talking to you."

"I will. I promise." I closed the door behind her and flipped the sign to closed.

I was going to make good on my promise. Adeline was a real friend outside of the spiritual world. She didn't have any expectations of me. She didn't know my real reasons for moving my cure shop from the flea market to here.

I blew my bangs out of my face and took a deep breath when I turned around to get a good look at Peony. She was next to the counter giving Mr. Prince Charming the rub of his life. I was hoping to talk to Madame Torres before I went to the smudging ceremony to see what she was glowing about. She glowed when she was mad, she glowed when she was happy, she glowed just to glow, so I wasn't sure if she had any information about my nightmares or why Mr. Prince Charming had given me the third eye charm. All I knew was that I was going to have to wait to talk to her until after the ceremony.

"I'm not sure about your village, but we don't really play the spiritual, witchy part with clothing. Its here that matters most." I tapped my finger to my heart. "And you can't go around talking about it in front of non-spiritualists."

"But I thought." She opened her mouth and shut it quickly when she looked at me and I was shaking my head.

"Regardless of who you think is safe and not safe, you never know," I warned giving her the benefit of the doubt because she was young and I remember how I felt when I came to Whispering Falls and didn't understand the spiritual rules or the impact of my actions on the village as a whole.

"Oh okay." She nodded her head, her eyes big.

"Now, let's get to making the smudging sticks." I went back to the counter pausing for a minute when I noticed my charm bracelet.

I touched each one happy to know Adeline had given me a little reprieve from the situation that could be looming over me. Danger. Death. Burning buildings.

"I love your bracelet," Peony said when we went around to the cauldron.

"Mr. Prince Charming gave it to me on my tenth birthday." I played with the turtle charm, missing one emerald eye stone. "This one was my first one. I had no idea he was my fairy-god cat and each charm was for protection. The turtle charm means courage, longevity, strength, protection, innocence, and patience. Everything I needed as a ten-year-old girl."

"Yeah." She shuffled the toe of her shoe on the tile floor while looking down. "That is the hardest part about this world. I have no idea if what I'm doing is right or wrong. Just like that." She pointed to the cauldron.

"Have you figured out your talent?" I asked. Her eyes crossed. "Your spiritual gift. Petunia's is talking to animals and afterlife."

"My cousin, Gwendolyn, she says I'm trying to figure it out. She says I'm not letting myself become what I'm supposed to become." She watched as I flipped the switch on the cauldron.

I sprayed the cleaner in and made it spic and span clean. There was no holds barred on tonight's ceremony since I had to put a protective smudge on the village, Mr.

Prince Charming gave me the charm, and my nightmares were getting more vivid.

"Your cousin is right." I ran my finger down the line of potions behind us and grabbed the bottle of Raspberry Leaves, Rosemary, and Verbena.

The Raspberry Leaves and Rosemary offered protection, while the Verbena was to bring peace. Both would be much appreciated at this time.

"You really think so?" She planted her hand on the counter and leaned on it.

"Yeah. You seem young and you have to let your gift grow. I didn't know I had a gift until a couple years ago." I wanted to make her feel better. "And I'm way older than you."

"Not by much. I'm twenty-one." She watched me intently as I started the mixture.

The oily tonic in the cauldron bubbled to a frothy mixture, perfect to dip the smudging bundle into and no one would ever know I had used an extra spell for Petunia's ceremony.

It was my way of slipping the protection in without alarming anyone.

"I have to apologize for Amethyst." Peony was a lot like Petunia. They both apologized for other's actions. "She is a little protective over Petunia. They've been friends a long time. They are like sisters."

"I wish she didn't judge me so much and I'm not really going to put a spell on her." I winked and slowly stirred the cauldron. The mixture needed to be a dull brown in color so it would blend in with the smudging bundle. "I guess I can't relate because I don't have any family or friends."

"It looks like you have a husband." Her eyes glanced at my ring.

"Oh yeah." Memories of Oscar getting down on his knee and asking me to marry him made my heart soar. So much so, I had almost forgotten about the evil lurking in the air. "Oscar is my family."

Mewl. Mr. Prince Charming growled.

"And you buddy!" I ran my hand down his fur before reaching on the shelf for the bundle of blue sage smudge sticks.

"That is what you wave around?" Peony was very interested.

I had a twinge of jealousy in me because she was young and had a big interest in learning.

"It is." I dipped the bundle in the cauldron, letting the protection mixture add to the protection the blue sage was already going to give to Petunia and her reign as Village President. "It will help Petunia keep a clear head."

"Amethyst told Petunia you shouldn't do the ceremony because you weren't strong enough to keep the presidency going," Peony said.

"Seriously? God, what a . . ." I bit my lip. "Maybe I should put a dash of something in here for Amethyst so she can keep her mouth shut."

I held the smudging stick over the cauldron to let the extra drip off. If Amethyst didn't reel her mouth in and change her attitude, Whispering Falls was going to be too small for the both of us.

"I'm sorry." I regretted saying that to Peony. "I shouldn't have said that. I don't like being judged by someone who doesn't even know me. You are kind and I can see you and Petunia are a lot alike."

Peony smiled. Her eyes forgiving and not another word was said about Amethyst.

The knock at the door got our attention and we peeked out from behind the partition.

Oscar stood on the doorstep. He looked a little cold. I snapped a clothespin and the smudge stick to the shelf so it would dry and walked over to the door.

"I'm starving and Colton said he and Ophelia were going to have to cancel tonight. Something about inventory at the book store." He pulled me into his arms and wrapped me into a warm hug. The cold air rushed behind him. "But me and you can grab a bite to eat after the ceremony. Maybe in Locust Grove?"

"Oh, yeah." There wasn't anything I wanted more than to be with Oscar and on a date.

Ahem. Peony cleared her throat from the back of the store.

"Peony." My face blushed. When I was around Oscar, the entire world seemed to melt away. "I'm sorry. This is my fiancé, Oscar Park." She walked toward us. I said, "Peony is Petunia's sister and here for to see Petunia take the Village President oath."

"Nice to meet you." Peony stuck her hand out and they shook. "I didn't realize you were engaged to the *sheriff.*"

"She is." Oscar informed her. He put his arm around my shoulder, giving me a squeeze.

Mr. Prince Charming darted out the door before Oscar could close it behind him.

"It's getting really cold out there. Unseasonably cold." Oscar did a shimmy shake. He removed his arm and blew into his hands before rubbing them together.

"I guess I better bundle up then." Peony headed to the door. "I will see you soon. And June," she briefly paused, "I'm sorry about Amethyst. She really is a great friend to my sister."

"No big deal." I waved it off. "I'm sure she's very protective of her."

"Nice to meet you," she and Oscar said in unison before she left the shop.

"I've been waiting all day to do this." I placed my hands on the back of his neck, pulling him to me. Our lips parted, greeting each other, moving in unison.

It was like we were meant for each other. Our bodies responding to each other, his hands pulling me as close as we could get. There was a dreamy intimacy to our kiss I was sure no one had ever felt but us.

"You are killing me," he groaned. His eyes closed, his hands roamed. "Maybe we should skip dinner and go back to your place after the ceremony."

"That does sound better." I tilted my head to the side, letting his lips sear down my neck.

"Get a room," a muffled Madame Torres spouted out from the depth of my bag. "I haven't got all day and right now would be a great time to discuss the ever present danger to you, June Heal."

"Danger?" Oscar pulled me away. "What danger?" He dragged me by the hand toward the glowing bag.

"You never know when to keep your mouth shut, do you?" I dug deep into the bag and pulled out my snarky crystal ball.

"What good is having a cop for your man if you aren't going to use him when needed?" She cocked her purple brow in the air. Her face stern. "You need to watch Petunia's family and friend. They do not have her or your best interests at heart."

"Amethyst?" Oscar asked.

"Yeah. We sort of mixed words today." I hated to admit I had let her get my goat.

"Colton said something about it. I figured it was a customer," he muttered uneasily.

"She isn't a big fan of me because I had been the Village President before." Suddenly I was regretting letting her get to me. "I probably should've walked away, but I had to defend myself."

"You don't have to worry about them. They will all be gone tomorrow," he assured me. "Now, what was Madame Torres saying about danger?"

"June has been having nightmares again." Madame Torres appeared. The blue water surrounding her became cloudy and images of me sleeping filled the ball. "She hasn't been sleeping well and it's affecting her on a daily basis."

"Madame Torres, since when did you become Oscar's familiar?" I was a little pissed she just blurted out whatever she wanted.

"Fine, but don't forget the part about Mr. Prince Charming giving you a new charm." Her ball went black.

"Charm? What?" Oscar's voice rose in surprise.

I sucked in a deep breath and grabbed the lighter. If we didn't get a move on, we were going to be late for the ceremony, then Amethyst would really be mean to me.

"It's nothing."

"Nothing?" He grabbed me by the arm to stop me from fiddling around. "Look at me," he ordered me. His eyes held concern. "I saw you last night. You were freaked out. How long have the nightmares been going on?"

"A month or so." I shrugged and jerked out of his grip. I sprayed the cauldron with cleaner and decided to leave it sit overnight. "I know what you are going to say. If I would have addressed this a month ago, we wouldn't be in this situation today."

"It obviously wasn't going to go away by you ignoring it for a month," he said the words that rang true. "They never just go away until they come true in some sort of way."

I listened to him rant and rave about all the other nightmares I had had and how they had come true. I grabbed generic potion bottles and began refilling the empty shelves from the day's sales. There wasn't going to be any time to make all the potions I needed to make.

Nervously, I walked around all the small tables in the center of the room, running my hands over the tablecloths that covered them, making sure everything was in order for opening tomorrow.

Smudging ceremonies were long and took a lot out of me, plus I was going to spend time with Oscar tonight, which meant I would be too tired to come in early to do all of the necessary things that needed to be done before I could open the shop.

"You are right. I should have told you," I said what he wanted to hear. "But I didn't so let's move on." I nodded and grabbed my bag. I put Madame Torres in the bottom.

Oscar grabbed my hand with my charm bracelet on my wrist.

He snapped his wand off his belt, which to most people looked like a billy club, and tapped the charm. Wizard school was teaching them how to use their wands in many situations other than casting spells.

"Third eye?" he questioned. "What is it you need clarification on? What is Mr. Prince Charming trying to protect you from?"

"I don't know." I hated to tell him that, but it was the truth. "Bella wasn't able to clarify for me. She said she felt it odd he picked the third eye. And I feel it." I put my hand on my gut and closed my eyes. "I feel danger. I feel evil. I smell death."

Chapter Seven

"Colton." As Oscar spoke into his police walkie-talkie, which was attached to his uniform on his shoulder, we made our way up the hill to The Gathering Rock. "Keep a look out while the town is at Petunia's inauguration. June feels evil is lurking."

"Got it," Colton's voice rang out of Oscar's microphone.

"Nothing to worry about." Oscar put his arm around my shoulders helping keep the chill at bay.

The Gathering Rock was up the hill near my cottage. It was a large rock and the gathering space where we held all of our ceremonies and celebrations.

"What is going on with the teenagers tonight?" Isadora Solstice noticed the fireflies swarming around Peony.

Isadora was the spiritualist who found Oscar and I in Locust Grove. She was the one who had brought us to Whispering Falls. She had always been so good to us.

She was the Village President for a long time. The fireflies in the village were sweet souls of teenagers who had passed from the living world into the spiritual world. Just like the living teenager, they loved to come out at night and stay up, bugging you in the process. They were probably in love with Peony and her youthful spirit.

"I'd like to wrap my fingers around her neck." Isadora's hazel eyes zeroed in on Gwendolyn who was silently standing beside Petunia. Her long lashes sweeping upward, she pushed her wavy blond hair from her face and straightened her shoulders.

Izzy was always dressed so impeccably. Today she wore an A-line skirt with a spider print, black turtleneck, and her pointy laced-up boots to compliment the hunter green cloak.

"She has made that impression on you too?" I asked.

Oscar didn't say anything. He knew we girls needed to gossip.

"She had the nerve to come into my shop and tell me I was doing it all wrong."

Mystic Lights was filled with beautiful lighting elements. Anyone would be grateful to have her amazing designs. Her spiritual talent was crystal ball reading and all things aura, light and love. She had a truly magical spirit. As one of the oldest village members, she was smart and talented.

Every time I looked at her, she reminded me of Meryl Streep, the actress. And she always held herself to the highest standards.

"She's a beast and I'm so glad they are leaving tomorrow." She lowered her eyes. "This village isn't big enough for the two of us."

"Who are you talking about?" Raven Mortimer asked. She turned her head to the side; her black ponytail flung around whipping around her face. "Let me guess. Gwendolyn?"

That was what I loved about Raven. She was fun, young and spoke her mind.

"She's the devil. It took everything I had not to throw a little something-something in that tart she's eating."

We all looked at Gwendolyn who was now stuffing the tasty pastry in her mouth. And we all knew what Raven meant by a little something-something.

"I couldn't agree more." Isadora rubbed her hands together. "I better take my seat."

"Are you feeling okay?" Constance Karima moseyed up to our little group.

Patience stood behind her, both with a curious look in their eyes. "Sick. Someone's gonna die." Patience's eyes grew with excitement.

"No one is going to die," I assured them.

"Yes. Yes there is." Constance rubbed her hands together with anticipation of the thought.

"Yes there is," Patience repeated and followed her sister to their seats in front of The Gathering Rock.

Raven and I watched Isadora go where the Village Council sat during the ceremonies. Behind The Gathering Rock. Izzy sat next to Gerald and Petunia.

"Gwendolyn had the nerve to tell me my tart was too . . .," she pursed her lips and sucked in, "too tart!

And she hated the June's Gem Petunia bought for her this morning."

"I think she hates the June." I pointed to myself. Out of the corner of my eye, I could see Patience Karima sniffing everyone who walked by her. "Gwendolyn thinks people should go to the doctor and not try silly little cures." I pounded my closed fist in my hand. "I wanted to knock her out. She even made fun of my shop. Colton had to step in."

"He did?" She gasped. "She's a nasty woman. Thank God she doesn't live here. She'd never make it."

"No joke." My voice was flat.

Raven and I quickly shut up when Gwendolyn passed by us. She didn't bother looking our way. Instead she bolted back down the hill with the tart in her grasp, Peony close behind her.

"IBS." Peony laughed, batting away the fireflies from her face.

"Excuse me?" I asked.

"Gwenie has IBS. Irritable Bowel Syndrome." She swatted more fireflies.

"Come on." I waved my hand in the air. "Let our guest be." The fireflies buzzed off. "Teenagers." I rolled my eyes. I turned to Raven. "How much time do we have?"

"About ten minutes." Her brows furrowed. "Why?"

There was probably more time than that. Villagers were still making their way up the hill.

"I'll be right back." I threw the edges of my cloak around my body to shield the cold as I darted back down the hill toward Gwenie.

Chapter Eight

"No, June!" Madame Torres yelled from the bottom of my bag. She flopped up and down like a rag doll with me running as fast as I could to get to Gwenie. If I got on her good side, maybe she could help me out with Amethyst.

I was good at ignoring Madame Torres from the depths of the bag. She insisted she got "bag sick", a sort of car sick. I had fell for her antics several times, but not tonight. I had Petunia's cousin to win over and if she had a bad case of irritable bowel syndrome, I had the perfect cure for it.

"June!" Madame Torres glowed a deep almost blood red.

"What?" I asked very loudly and looked into the bag.

Truth, potion, deceptive, manipulative. The words floated in her ball.

"What do these words mean?" I asked her, trying to decipher her new way of communicating with me.

"How do I know?" Her red lips appeared in the black liquid within the ball. "I'm just bringing you *what I see, what I feel*." She was so dramatic. "You are the one who is supposed to know what they mean! How did I get such a dumb spiritualist?"

"Watch it," I warned and shut my bag up. I looked up and Gwenie was almost to town. "Gwendolyn!" I yelled down the hill and ignored my crystal ball. "Gwenie!"

She stopped in front of A Cleansing Spirit Spa. Chandra Shango, owner and palm reader, had her key in the door of the shop and stood there with a dumbfounded look on her face. Chandra wasn't going anywhere. She was a nosy as they come.

"I think June Heal is trying to get your attention," Chandra said to Gwendolyn in her warm and inviting voice.

With curious eyes, Chandra watched intently while adjusting her orange and pink turban with the large purple feather sticking out of the back on her head.

"I'm Chandra Shango, owner of A Cleansing Spirit Spa." Chandra stuck her hand out for Gwendolyn to shake. Only Chandra flipped it over, getting a good glance at Gwendolyn's palm, quickly dropping it. "Oh dear." Chandra hurried off in the direction of The Gathering Rock. "I'm going to be late for the ceremony." She grabbed me on my way over to Gwendolyn. "You come with me."

"No," I pulled out of her grip, "I want to talk to Gwenie and I'll be right there."

"I really think it's best you come with me, June." Chandra's sweet voice was stern. Her hazel eyes hardened and she nervously picked at the edges of her raspberry hair; her nail color matched.

"My close family and friends call me Gwenie. Not you." Gwenie's words shot at me like an arrow, her eyes glowed, and brows lifted. "What do you want to see me about?" she questioned.

"It was brought to my attention your IBS is acting up and I wanted to extend an olive branch and offer you a special remedy passed down from spiritual generation to spiritual generation." I pointed to my shop right next door. "It's just right inside."

"I think we should go." Chandra tugged on me again.

"Fine." Gwenie made the first step toward my shop. "But I think my stomach is gurgling from nerves of the opening of Full Moon, and Petunia's ceremony. Not some silly little diagnosis with IBS."

"I will be right there." I put my hands in front of Chandra to stop her from touching me. "It will only take a second. And the cure will help a nervous stomach."

"If you give me some sort of bad potion, you will regret the day you met me." Gwenie had evil coming out of every pore.

"If I had any sense, I would," I whispered cocking a brow to Chandra.

"I'm out of here." Chandra gave me one last chance. "Come on with me. Deal with her later."

"No. I'm dealing with her now. She's been nasty to everyone we love and maybe my little cure will bring relief to us all." I waved her off and met Gwenie at the gate of A Charming Cure.

"Is everything okay?" Petunia was now standing next to Chandra.

"Fine." I waved her off. "I'm going to help her feel better." I smiled and turned back to Gwenie.

Reluctantly, Chandra and Petunia turned to go up to The Gathering Rock.

"I don't know why are you trying to be nice to me. I'm leaving tomorrow." Gwenie planted her hand on her hips. "I see no good coming from this. No good whatsoever. And after tomorrow, you will probably never see me again."

"Why would you say such a thing?" I asked and used my key to open the door.

Once inside, I flipped on the lights. My shop reflected my pride; I had come a long way from the flea market booth and I was proud of what I had continued from my parents.

Illuminated by the hanging chandeliers throughout the shop, the ornamental glass bottles glistened like magic in the dim light. Each display table in the middle of the room had a red tablecloth covering that fell to the floor. Romantic and beautiful. It truly took my breath away.

"You have no idea of the family secrets held in any family other than yours." Gwenie's eyes dropped.

"Every family has their own secrets." My face softened. "Trust me, I know all about that."

I wasn't going to waste the precious time I had, not to mention the few minutes, to go into detail how Oscar's uncle had been the evil force behind the death of my parents and Oscar's. It was a secret better left buried.

"We are lucky, you know." I gave a sympathetic smile. She wasn't going to spill about the family issues and I wasn't going to push. "Magic isn't seen by the untrained eye, but magic binds us together. We are blessed to share the bond."

"You are right. I'm so sorry I judged Whispering Falls. Our village isn't so," she paused. Her throat moved up and down as she gulped. "Isn't so helpful. We have some really nasty, selfish citizens."

I gave her another sympathetic look. This was one time I was glad I didn't have to deal with negative people. My life was good and I had a wonderful community to foster the goodness in all.

"Now." I hurried back to the counter for the special potion. I tapped each bottle, one by one, down the shelf. Nothing lit up. "Hmm." Perplexed, I tapped down the line again.

Nothing.

"It has to be here somewhere," I said. "It has all sorts of good homeopathic stuff in it. Slippery elm and aloe juice will help reduce any inflammation. Chamomile tea leaves crushed up in the mixture will soothe and help repair damage. Rosemary, peppermint, catnip, fennel, and green drinks are also excellent choices for colon health. So if you go by The Gathering Grove on your way home in the morning, I'm sure your cousin-in-law will fix you right up."

I glanced around for the bottle I knew I had made up. I specifically put it in a clear bottle with an ornamental wire wrapped around it. Plus the cork lid was gorgeous. There was *nothing* beautiful about bowel problems, so I wanted the lucky recipient to have a nice bottle to look at.

"Oh!" I was excited to find the bottle. It was hidden behind the Lonely Heart Potion. I grabbed it, noticing it didn't light up to my touch. The clock on the wall told me I didn't have time to make a new potion, but I knew this one was it. "Here is it."

I brushed away any doubt and handed her the bottle.

"This is pretty." Gwendolyn said her first nice thing to me.

"Thank you. Meant for you." I placed my hands over her hands and became dizzy. The smell of charred ashes enveloped me. I leaned on a display table gathering my wits. "Let's go."

"I'm going to go back to Petunia's and go to the bathroom," she said when I flipped off the light and headed out the door. "I have a few minutes before you start the inauguration right?"

"Yes." I nodded trying to put the smell in the back of my head. It was difficult, as it was taking over my nose, my lungs, and my heart. "I'll be sure to watch for you before I start."

I darted down the steps and around the shop. I looked up at the hill where everyone was waiting for me to start the ceremony. I sucked in a deep breath, clearing out my lungs, my head, my soul.

Suddenly, I became very tired. As if something had zapped all of my energy.

Just like that. My intuition hit me.

There was a heavy cloud of evil looming over The Gathering Rock.

I looked back to make sure Gwenie had made it to Glorybee, but she must've really had to go to the bathroom. There was no time to make haste. The thickness of the evil was restricting my lungs. Whispering Falls was under attack. But from whom?

Everyone was gathered around the rock when I arrived.

"Please form a circle and hold hands," I instructed them and lit the smudging ritual candle, sitting on The Gathering Rock. "Today our smudge sticks incorporate mountain sage, cedar, and sweetgrass. This makes them perfect for rituals of purification, cleansing, and banishing to help Petunia begin her journey as Village President of Whispering Falls."

There was a crowd gathered behind Petunia. They seemed to be lowly chanting their own ritual, which wasn't unusual for families of other villages. There was no wrong or right way to bless and encourage a spiritual loved one. It was something I wasn't used to because I didn't have the pleasure of knowing my biological spiritual family.

I had to rely on my intuition and guidance on how to perform the ceremony the spiritual world wanted me to perform.

I lit the sage, fanning it with the eagle's wing to get the smoke rolling from the bundle.

Once the smoke was flowing out and I knew the protection potion the bundle was dipped in had also been ignited, I walked on the outside of the circle and fanned the group ending at Petunia. I let the smoke surround her from head to toe and proceeded around the outside of the circle until I stood in the middle.

"Every eye closed with good intentions to be sent up to the spiritual world to keep and help Petunia on her journey as Village President."

Once everyone had closed their eyes, I walked up to Petunia. She grinned, pride on her face. I tilted my head to the side and gave a happy nod. She was glowing.

The fireflies buzzed around her and many of the spiritualists who had come back in the form of an animal spirit stood behind her in line five hundred feet long, extending into the woods nestled behind The Gathering Rock.

"You are so lucky to have so many people here supporting you. Loving you." I felt a little envious.

When Isadora inducted me as the Village President, only the citizens of Whispering Falls had come.

"Thank you so much, June." She took in a deep breath, letting out a happy sigh. "You have been a very good friend."

"Let's begin." I sucked in a deep breath through my nose, losing all the senses around me, focusing only on Petunia and her need to have the most protection. Everything around me disappeared.

I lifted the bundle in the air. In long swift motions, I ran the eagle's wing through the bundle's smoke, creating an abnormal amount of smoke into the air.

My voice boomed throughout the nighttime air as I changed the smudging prayer for Petunia, "May your hands be cleansed; that they create beautiful things. May your feet be cleansed; that they may take you where you most need to be. May your heart be cleansed; that you might hear its message clearly. May your throat be cleansed; that you might speak rightly; when words are needed. May your eyes be cleansed; that you might see the signs; and wonders of this world. May this person and space be washed clean by the smoke of these fragrant plants. And may that same smoke carry our prayers, spiraling, to the Heavens. All acts of Love and Pleasure are my Rituals."

I fanned more and more as I spoke the prayer, hoping the extra protection potion circled her and engulfed her soul.

It must've been overboard because everyone around me coughed bringing me out of my focus. All my surroundings came back to me. Smoke was everywhere.

I threw the smudge on the ground and patted it out with the toe of my shoe, wondering if the extra potion had caused the great amount of smoke in the air.

"Thank you, June." Petunia fanned her hand in front of her face, parting some of the fumes between us.

"I'm sorry." I cackled. "I must've gotten carried away."

A shrill shriek made me jump around.

"No!" Chandra screamed, pointing down the hill.

As if in slow motion, my eyes slid down her arm, to the tip of her finger, bouncing to the distance where she was pointing. The top of A Charming Cure was alight on fire. Smoke rolling out of the roof.

"Mr. Prince Charming!" I screamed, dropping the feather and running down the hill as fast as I could.

Images of my nightmare flooded my head. Fright and panic engulfed me.

"Mr. Prince Charming!" I screamed and darted around to the front of the burning shop.

Without even thinking about my safety, I flung the gate open and kicked in the front door. Smoke poured out. Thick as fog, I couldn't see through it.

"June! Stop!"

I could hear Oscar behind me, only I couldn't stop. My fairy-god cat had always been there for me and I was going to be there for him.

Chapter Nine

"Mr. Prince Charming isn't in there." Oscar knelt down beside me; I sat on the sidewalk outside of the shop. He rubbed his hand down my hair. "And the fire is now out, so we are going to try to go up to the attic to see what caught on fire."

"Okay." I bit my lip and looked around me.

"At least the bottom of your shop looks like it wasn't too damaged." Chandra's head tilted to the side trying to get a good look inside A Charming Cure's propped open door. Her turban nearly fell off before she fixed it. "I'm sure Mr. Prince Charming is safe."

"I wouldn't doubt it if he was napping on my tree," Petunia said.

Mr. Prince Charming was notorious for visiting Glorybee. He loved the animals and the live tree in the middle of her shop. If it didn't seem so strange, I would say Mr. Prince Charming had a fondness for a certain hedgehog in Petunia's shop.

"Can you go see if Mr. Prince Charming is in the shop?" Petunia asked Peony.

Woooo, woooooo.

The sound of ambulance siren got everyone's attention. In the distance, the Karima sisters' ambulance-turned-hearse-turned-ambulance, came barreling down the street. Lights and siren going, it came to an abrupt stop in front of the shop.

Constance jumped out of the driver's side as Patience hopped out of the passenger side. Both of them scurried to the back of their car and opened the back doors, rolling the cart out and snapping the locks in place.

"Outta the way!" Constance screamed, not caring about who was in front of her. "Fresh body to get!"

"Fresh body!" Patience pushed the gurney from behind and Constance had the front.

"There is no fresh body here." Oscar stood up and put his hand out in front of him to stop them. "Attic fire."

"There is a dead body." Constance tried to shove past him.

"No." Oscar took his cop stance, resting his hands on his hips.

"Oscar," Colton's voice came across the walkie-talkie on Oscar's shoulder. "I think you need to come up here. I found a body."

"Told ya." Constance by-passed Oscar.

She and Patience jerked the gurney up the steps like it was nothing. Oscar shoved past them, bolting up the stairs.

"What?" I cried out, trying to sort the words out in my head.

I jumped up, Bella grabbed one of my arms, Chandra the other.

"I wonder?" Chandra directed her question at me. "I saw it June." Her voice hardened. "It was in her palm when I shook her hand before you coerced her into getting a potion from you. I saw her death."

"Who? Gwenie?" I begged to know. There was a jolt of sickness covering my entire body. "You mean to tell me Gwendolyn Shrubwood is in there dead?" I questioned in a hushed tone.

"I warned you." Chandra nervously played with her turban.

"Oh no, June. Don't tell me you had Gwendolyn in your shop," Bella paused, *"alone."*

I closed my eyes, trying to get a breath to calm myself. My intuition flooded my being. Jittery was best how I could describe the feeling deep in my bones.

"June?" Izzy stepped up. "What is going on?"

"I think Gwendolyn Shrubwood is dead in my shop." I bit my lip and took off toward the shop. I couldn't stand it any longer.

"You aren't going anywhere." Bella's voice was dark, cold and it scared me. "You stay right here where everyone can see you."

"Is it her?" I asked, looking around, trying to find her face in the crowd. She wasn't anywhere.

All the people I knew and loved were next to me. Every shop owner was there. Gerald and Arabella stood with Petunia and her family. Ophelia kept her distance on the steps of Ever After Books. Raven and Faith stood

with her.

"Mr. Prince Charming wasn't in there." Peony came

back, out of breath. "What's going on?"

"Colton found a body," Petunia held tight to

Amethyst.

"Dead body?" Peony's voice cracked. "Surely not."

Petunia's face dropped.

We stood there in silence waiting for anyone to walk

out of my cure shop. It seemed like it was hours, but in

reality, it was only a few minutes before Oscar walked

out. He took his cop's hat off his head and rubbed his

hands through his hair. Ruffling it a bit.

His blue eyes stared at me, making my gut ache. It

wasn't good news. He knew something. Something bad. I

ran my hand over my wrist. If I could use some

protection, it would be now. And I definitely could use

Mr. Prince Charming by my side.

Oscar walked past me and stopped in front of

Petunia.

"Petunia," his voice was almost a whisper, "I hate to bring you such bad news on your celebratory day, but your cousin Gwendolyn is dead."

Petunia fell to the ground, Gerald catching her.

"Dead?" Amethyst stepped up. "What do you mean dead?"

"When Officer Lance did a sweep of the attic after the fire was put out, her body was found on his search." Oscar held his hat tight to his body. "There doesn't seem to be any obvious cause. Was there a reason she'd be in A Charming Cure?"

"Her." Amethyst's finger stabbed my way.

Oscar glanced over. Slowly his eyes closed as though his heart sank.

"She had to be the last one to see Gwenie. After all," Amethyst's words were bitter. "Little Miss Heal had mixed words with Gwenie, not to mention she just so happened to have wanted to *help* with her IBS. Didn't you?"

"I. . .I," I stuttered. "She left my shop alive. I locked the door behind. . ." I stopped when I realized I didn't lock the door. I was in a hurry to get to the smudging ceremony. "I didn't mean anything by my words. Hell," I pointed to Izzy, "she said she wanted to strangle her. And Raven," I moved my finger down the street to Wicked Good, "she said Gwenie put down her tarts. It wasn't just me she offended."

"Don't say another word," Bella warned. "Wait until Mac McGurtle gets here."

"Mac?" I questioned. "Why do I need Mac?"

Mac McGurtle was my childhood neighbor when I was growing up in Locust Grove. Though I had found out, he was really a spiritualist who had been summoned by the Elders to live next door to me and Darla to make sure we were safe.

"He was assigned to you as your spiritual guide as a kid and you kept him all your life." Bella shook her head. "Something is fishy and Mac will get to the bottom of it."

"There is no evidence June or anyone had anything to do with the death of your cousin." Oscar made sure to keep Gwenie's family and friend a safe distance from me. "The Karima sisters will do an autopsy to see if there was any funny business."

"Move it! Dead body coming through!" Constance screamed, the gurney rolling at a fast speed behind her.

"Dead body! Fresh dead body!" Patience beamed with joy.

Chapter Ten

Everyone stood still in silence. An uncomfortable silence.

Colton said a few things to Oscar; then Oscar came over and kissed me on the forehead, whispering he'd meet me at the cottage after he went to visit his Aunt Eloise and let her know what was going on because Colton wanted her to do a cleansing sweep tonight at midnight and the next several nights to come.

Colton stood next to Petunia who was circled in the comfort of all her family members.

"Her!" Amethyst screamed rushing toward me. "You threatened her today when she made it known she would rather go to a doctor than try one of your little Betty Crocker herbs."

"Now, now." Petunia had tears in her eyes. "June would never do anything like that."

"You are in charge now!" Amethyst yelled at Petunia, reminding me of my failure. "Use your presidential power to arrest her. Demand the sheriff to arrest her."

"Actually," Izzy swept across the sidewalk, her skirt swooshed. "The ceremony was not complete and June is still the Village President.

"I'm so sorry." It was ridiculous for anyone to think I could hurt someone, much less kill her. My heart was breaking for Petunia. I reached out to touch her; Amethyst shoved between us. I sucked in a deep breath to calm my nerves. "What can I do to help you?"

"Nothing." Petunia shook her head, tears dripped down her face. Gerald wrapped her in his arms and she broke out into a full-blown cry. He picked her up and carried her to Glorybee. Peony and Amethyst walked behind them.

Everyone watched with deep sadness. Amethyst opened the door of Glorybee and glanced back to me. She glared at me with a burning, reproachful eye before she disappeared into the shop.

"June," Colton walked up next to me. "I am going to have to ask you a few questions."

"I didn't kill her." I was shocked at how angry my words sounded.

"I didn't accuse you of anything, but this is your shop and I feel it is necessary I take over as the lead detective since you *are* engaged to Oscar." His eyes were hard when he looked at Oscar who confirmed what he was saying. "And I don't think you are going to be able to open the shop for some time. The attic has some fire damage, but the rest of the shop looks fine."

"But I have bills to pay like everyone else." Suddenly, the realization my shop was damaged hit me hard. I rubbed my charm bracelet wishing Mr. Prince Charming would show up.

"Don't worry about any bills." Bella put a comforting arm around me. "We will take one day at a time." She patted me.

Raven walked up with a small paper bag.

"I thought you might want a little treat." She handed me the bag.

Our eyes caught. For a second, her eyes grew and sent a dart to my gut. She'd had some sort of reading in the dough of the June's Gem she had made.

I gulped and brushed a strand of hair behind my ear.

"Thank you." I said and nodded, letting her know I knew she wanted to talk to me.

She gave a slight smile.

"Let me know if I can do anything." She turned and headed to her bakery.

"Can you come to the station?" Colton asked.

"Sure," I answered and turned to Chandra. "If you see Mr. Prince Charming, can you please tell him to come to the station?"

"Yes, dear." Chandra reached out and touched my hand. She flipped it over and ran her long blue and star-painted fingernail down my palm. "I warned you not to help her."

Panic like I had never felt before churned in my gut. Chandra's earlier words did warn me not to go into the shop, but stubborn me wanted Gwenie to like me so much, I wasn't going to listen to anyone. Not even my intuition.

Colton gave me the let's go look and we walked across the street to the station. It was a typical station, not like the rest of the buildings in Whispering Falls. It was pretty institutional looking with a glass window front and two desks on the inside. The back of the station was where Oscar lived. Colton lived with Ophelia in the apartment on top of the bookstore.

"You can sit there." Colton pointed to one of the two chairs in front of his desk.

I took a seat and looked around for Oscar. He wasn't there but Mac McGurtle was, his briefcase gripped in his thick fingers. His blue eyes frowned behind his black large-rimmed eyeglasses.

"Mac," I stood back up, happy to see him. I hugged him a bit tighter than normally.

It was good to see someone from my past that I had known as far back as I could remember. He gave me comfort, easing my soul a little more.

"I came as fast as I could." He took out a handkerchief from his suit coat pocket and rubbed the sweat from his brow. "I came all the way from Florida."

"Florida?" I asked.

"Yes, I was checking into Petunia's family members. I had no idea she hailed from a village from the sunshine state." He sat down and plunked his briefcase on the desk in front of him. "Now, is my client being charged with the murder of Gwendolyn Shrubwood?"

"No, but I can't help but have some questions about her feelings for Ms. Shrubwood since I did hear them having a disagreement earlier," Colton informed him of the conversation he had overheard in front of The Gathering Grove.

"Madame Torres, please." Mac held his hand out.

I dug deep in my bag and grabbed her.

"Thank you, Mac." Madame Torres heaved like she had been suffocated. "I've been dying to get out of the bottom of her nasty bag all day long. The trash." She shook her head. The water surrounding her hit the side of the glass ball like a tsunami.

"Seriously?" I put her down with a little more of a thump than normal, making her head bump to the top of the glass.

"Okay, ladies." Mac slid Madame Torres over in front of him. "Please play back the scene Colton Lance saw this morning between June and Gwendolyn."

Her head twisted in the water toward me. I nodded in approval; happy she did check with me first before she played out the scene. After all, she was mine.

Like a movie, Madame Torres played back. I had forgotten how Gwendolyn accused me of stealing the Village President position from Petunia. Petunia was visibly upset as Gwendolyn recalled how I had come to the village and was handed the job.

Colton and Mac both wrote down things on paper as the scene played out.

"I think she was really trying to take up for her cousin who had been hurt, but that doesn't give good reason for me to kill her," I spoke with confidence.

"At the scene, Petunia said Gwenie didn't make it to the ceremony, but a few minutes before she rushed down to see where Gwenie went." Colton flipped through his notebook. "You and Gwenie were getting ready to go into A Charming Cure, assuring her you'd be there in a minute. She also said Chandra was talking to you, so I need to go over to see her and get her take on it."

"Yes. Chandra, Gwenie and I were standing there. I was told Gwenie had IBS." I reiterated what I had learned. "Gwenie admitted her stomach was upset and I have a great family remedy for it."

"I'm going to need the remedy." Colton shoved a pencil and piece of paper in front of me.

I quickly wrote down the herbs I used and gave her.

"Nothing special." I shrugged. "I was just trying to help."

"That's a crime?" Mac asked, sitting back in the chair and folding his hands in front of him.

"No. But I'd like to know what you two were discussing." Colton leaned in, not letting Mac intimidate him.

"Can I?" I looked over at Mac.

He lifted his hand toward Colton, gesturing me to go on.

"She had been a bit nasty to me and I wanted her to like me." I recalled the conversation. "She said I didn't know her family dynamics and I needed to butt out. She also said she couldn't wait until she got home and her village was nothing like ours. That was it. We left."

"And?" Colton lifted a brow, clicked the small tape recorder in front of him and slid it toward the edge of the desk, near me.

"She asked me why I was being nice to her since she was so nasty to me and I told her I wanted to help. She told me to stay out of her family business because I didn't know everything. I didn't go into detail, but I told her we all had our own share of family issues."

I stopped when tears came to my eyes. Mac gave me his sweaty handkerchief and I took it anyway. I wiped my tears and continued.

"Before we went into the shop, Chandra told me not to go. Ask her. She read something in Gwenie's palm when they shook hands." I wanted to make sure they were clear on the fact I didn't do any funny business. "Plus Gwenie was mean to Izzy. Ask Izzy. She even said she wanted to strangle Gwenie. And," I knew I was ratting out everyone, but I had to look out for me. "Raven even said she was mad because Gwenie said her tarts were too tart."

"What was in the cure?" Colton asked as though he hadn't hears a word I'd said about the others.

"Let's see." The best I could under the nervous circumstances I was in, I read my list I had just written down for him, "Slippery elm and aloe juice for inflammation. Chamomile tea leaves helps repair damage. I also told her to grab a Rosemary, peppermint, catnip, fennel, or green drink from Gerald on her way out of town in the morning because it was also good for colon health." I threw my hands in the air. "See, nothing damaging. All good stuff." I pushed the paper back toward him.

"And you never mixed anything up in the cauldron?" he asked.

I shook my head.

"The last thing I had made in my cauldron was for a little boy—a no more gossip potion and confidence potion in one I called *Monsters Be Gone*." I shrugged. "In fact, I had cleaned my cauldron and replaced all the potions that had sold out today."

"That's interesting." Colton leaned back in his chair tapping the butt end of his pen to his temple. "Because when I went in the burning shop to put it out," he tapped his wand, "your cauldron was bubbling full."

"No, it couldn't have been," I assured him.

He stood up and pulled a vial out of his pant's pocket.

"I even took a sample." He sat the small glass next to Madame Torres for me to get a good look.

The movie screen of today's events floated away from Madame Torres and a skull and crossbones filled her entire crystal ball. It wasn't the image that stuck my gut, it was the words floating in her ball that caught my breath.

Chapter Eleven

"June Heal, did you poison Ms. Gwendolyn Shrubwood?" Colton's voice boomed out, his finger pointing at me.

"No!" My head shook side-to-side, protesting. "No!"

"Say nothing else, June," Mac instructed me and shoved his chair back using his hand pushing off the desk to do it. "Are you arresting her?"

If Colton arrested me, I wouldn't be able to leave my cottage.

Colton shook his head no.

"My client is innocent until proven guilty. She will be in Locust Grove at her old residence until further notice."

Mac grabbed me. I scooped up Madame Torres and let Mac drag me out of the station.

"June," Faith Mortimer stuck a tape recorder in my face as soon as we walked out of the station. "Do you have any comments about the fire in your cure shop

today and the fact someone was found dead in your
attic?"

"No, Faith." I pushed her hand out of my face.

"Our readers would love to know!" She thrust the
recorder in my face again. "The talk around town is that
you killed Gwendolyn Shrubwood. Any comments?"

"No!" I screamed, furious to be considered a
murderer. "Get out of my way," I murmured through my
gritted teeth.

*"Hear yea, hear yea, good subscribers of the
Whispering Falls Gazette,"* I could hear Faith's voice
echoing all over the town in the night air.

Faith was in charge of our spiritual newspaper. Only
spiritualists who subscribe for the paper could hear the
news and news flashes delivered through the air.
Tonight's event was obviously a news flash and I was the
center of it.

*"It's been unfortunate how one of our own, our
leader, June Heal will be relocating her cure shop to
Locust Grove until the storm blows over. When I went
around asking local merchants their take on where June*

Heal killed Petunia's cousin Gwendolyn Shrubwood, one local merchant quoted June Heal in saying 'I'm dealing with her now.' Her being Gwendolyn. And June continued to say how Gwendolyn had been nasty to everyone we love and maybe my little cure will bring relief to us all. Stay tuned to the Gazette to find out more about this ongoing murder investigation. Be sure to tell your family and friends to subscribe to the Whispering Falls Gazette. This issue was brought to you by A Charming Cure. Stop in today to get your . . ." Faith paused. *"I guess you won't be stopping in today."*

"Oh my God!" I fumed and stormed up the hill with Mac next to me. Madame Torres flopped around in the bottom of my bag that I'd strapped across my shoulder. "I did not kill her or give her any bad potion. Chandra knew that."

"Chandra?" Mac asked, he huffed and puffed his round body to the porch of my cottage.

"Yes. She's the one I told about giving Gwendolyn a potion to help everyone. Remember, it was to make her IBS feel better which in turn should make her mood better—not no pulse, dead better." I opened the door hoping to find Mr. Prince Charming there.

He wasn't.

"So," I stepped inside my cozy home and shut the door. "Do I really have to go back to Locust Grove?"

"Yes." Mac's tone was definite. "I think it will be best until the Karima sisters do their autopsy and Petunia's family leaves." He looked out the kitchen window. "And fast if you don't mind."

I glanced out the window over his shoulder. Several lit torches dotted the night air, getting closer and closer to my home.

"What in the world?" My eyes squinted, trying to see into the darkness.

"Arrest June Heal!" the crowd screamed as they marched up the hill with Petunia leading the pack.

"I don't need anything but this." I grabbed my Magical Cures Book, passed down from my mother, off the coffee table along with my car keys. "Let's go!"

Mac and I wasted no time getting into my 1988 two-toned green El Camino.

"Get her!" someone in the crowd yelled. They took off running toward the El Camino. With my foot pushed down, the tires squealed, throwing dust clouds up behind us. I didn't bother looking back until we were safely out of Whispering Falls's town limits.

Chapter Twelve

"I'll be a son of a gun." I pulled my car into the driveway of my childhood home in Locust Grove and there he sat.

Mr. Prince Charming. He knew it and I should've not worried about where he was. I knew he would show up sometime. Routinely I forgot he was my fairy-god familiar, not the other way around.

"Sometimes you have to trust the magical world to work itself out." Mac reached over and patted my hand. "Just like your house. Primrose knew exactly what he was doing when he told you he was selling your house, when in fact, we didn't. Everything is the same as you left it."

Axelrod Primrose was the spiritualist realtor who was in charge of selling my house in Locust Grove when I moved to Whispering Falls.

"Now, we did rent it out, but they are gone and we put all your stuff back in the house." Mac's voice softened, "It was his last task."

"He is missed." I recalled the day I met Axelrod and how the whole transition to Whispering Falls was not only magical, but easy. "I still can't believe he is dead."

"Me either." Mac took a deep breath; using his thick fingers he pushed his glasses up on his nose. "And I'm going to be right over there at my house if you need me."

"I do need you." I wasn't going to lie. I was a marked woman and the little crowd with torches told me so. "I need you to figure out what happened to Gwenie. Why was she in my attic? How did she die?"

"You go in and rest." He opened the door. "I'll be over to visit later."

"Thanks." I sat in the Green Machine, the name I lovingly called my car, and watched Mac run through the herb garden between our houses.

A couple of years ago, I would have darted out of my little shed in the backyard and given Mac McGurtle a good cussing for traipsing through my herbs. Not today. My heart and soul felt better knowing he was just a few feet away.

I looked back at my charred shed in the side yard. The last time I was in there, I was concocting a homeopathic cure from Darla's "recipe book", which turned out to be the Magical Cures Book with all the life lessons I needed to know about. Needless to say, I mixed two herbs that didn't agree with each other and boom! My shed went up in a small explosion. The walls and glass windows were still intact, but the roof was gone.

I grabbed my bag and the book and got out of the car. Mr. Prince Charming didn't bother giving me a little fairy anything. His hind leg stuck straight up in the air and he cleaned his under carriage.

"You could've warned me you were here." I stomped up the front steps of home.

I turned around and looked across the street. All my childhood memories of Oscar Park and his uncle came flooding back when I looked at his house and the big tree out front.

A smile crossed my face. His uncle might have killed my family, but the memories of Oscar and me were happy ones. Especially the times we sat under that tree, downing the Ding Dongs until we passed out from the sugar high. Darla was fit to be tied when she found out I was feasting on sugar and not the vegetables she wanted me to eat.

My childhood wasn't magical like my life now. Darla worked her hinny off in order to put the stale bread and manager special foods from the grocery store on the table. The meat we cooked on the grill wasn't bloody red, it was milky brown and a day expired. Darla cooked them charred to make sure E. coli wasn't going to get us.

Still, it was my childhood and I didn't know any different until my tenth birthday when Mr. Prince Charming showed up on the same step he was sitting on today.

"Let's go." I took a deep breath. I put my key in the door and hand on the door knob.

Mewl, Mr. Prince Charming darted in a figure eight around my ankles letting me know it was okay to go in.

I opened the door with a little push, letting the door fully open. The light flooded inside. Mr. Prince Charming jumped up on the old radiator that sat just inside the door, taking his post like he used to.

I gave him a little scratch on top of his head when I stepped through the door. He batted at my charm bracelet.

"Yes, I believe in you and keeping me safe." My lips formed a thin line.

Though I really wanted to believe, I was afraid the signs were all pointing at me. I wished I could take back the day and my words. I wished I had listened to Chandra and gone up to the ceremony. I wished, I wished, I wished Gwenie was still alive.

She wasn't.

And all the fingers pointed to me. Was Petunia still so mad at me, she had been planning to seek her revenge on me the day I was stepping down as the president?

Of course Petunia and I had a few words when she felt I had snatched the presidency right out from under her, but I had thought we had come to a mutual truce. Things had been going well. Her wedding was gorgeous. And Oscar asked me to marry him. Things couldn't have been better.

"Whoa," the door opened back up when I tried to close it. Oscar stood on the other side with his toe pushing the bottom of the door back open, a brown sack in his hand.

I didn't have to ask or smell to know what was in it.

"I thought since we were here, we could eat like old times." Oscar stepped into the house.

Meowwww. Mr. Prince Charming smacked the bag.

"Of course I got you an egg roll." Oscar pulled the sack away.

Mr. Prince Charming jumped off the radiator and we followed Oscar down the hall and into the kitchen.

My eyes wandered over Oscar's back end. His jeans fit in all the right places. He wore a black tee that wasn't too tight or too loose. His biceps formed without him flexing, sending my emotions into overdrive. The last time we were in this house, our relationship was purely platonic. My, how things had changed.

"You know." I touched his biceps. He put the food on the farm table and turned around. I ran my hands through his black hair and rested my hands on his shoulders. He put his hands on my waist and pulled me tight. "I couldn't do this without you."

He picked me up and carried me back to my bedroom. The small twin bed still had the same unicorn and rainbow comforter cover on it. Gently he eased me down onto the bed. His hands unbuttoned my jeans and lifted my shirt over my head. His fingers were icy cold, but his palm was fiery hot. I returned the favor, taking my time with every snap of his button-fly jeans. He stood up and pulled his black shirt over his head, exposing his washboard stomach. Aroused now, I tugged his hand and pulled him down; letting his hands explore the soft lines of my chest, waist and hips.

A slight gasp escaped my lips as our bodies moved together in an exquisite harmony. Neither of us said anything. We let our bodies do all the talking. One to the other. We knew what each other wanted.

All the troubles of the day melted away as we let the contentment and peace flow between us.

"I love you, June." Oscar snuggled his nose in the nape of my neck. His lips seared a path up and moved his mouth over mine, devouring its softness.

His kiss sent spirals of ecstasy through me, rendering me helpless against his masterful seduction.

Chapter Thirteen

Oscar's hands moved gently up and down my back, melting away the day's tension, though the events still nested front and center of my brain. I curled into the curve of his body, wrapping his arms around me.

"Thank you for being here," I said, hugging his arms. "I was afraid you were going to stay in Whispering Falls getting the scoop on what was going on."

"Colton and I feel it's in our best interest for me to not be on the case at all." His deep voice whispered in my ear. "He is a good detective. He will find out what really happened."

"Mac said the same thing." My stomach growled. "What on earth am I going to do all day? Here?"

"One sec." Oscar jumped out of bed and stuck his finger out.

He pulled his jeans back on, leaving the buttons still unbuttoned. A smile crossed my face. I knew what was underneath those jeans and I couldn't contain my giddiness.

He came back with the bag of Chinese food in his grip. He crawled back in bed.

"Here is something we haven't ever done." He took out the cartoons and flattened the sack. "Let's eat."

Mr. Prince Charming jumped up on the bed.

"Thank goodness you aren't like a real cat." I peeled off a piece of my egg roll and gave it to him.

Of course normal cats can't eat people food, especially chocolate, but Mr. Prince Charming wasn't any old normal cat.

"I have an idea." Oscar stuffed his mouth with a piece of broccoli. "Why don't we fix the shed and you make some cures and get your booth back at the flea market?"

"What?" A nervous laugh escaped me.

"You heard me. You loved going to the flea market. And it just so happened that on my way to the Chinese joint, I stopped by the flea market and they have your old booth space available." He used the chopsticks to jam a few pieces of chicken in his mouth.

"Do you think I will be here that long?" The realization hit me like a brick.

"The autopsy might take a few days and you need to keep busy." He picked up the egg roll and held it to my lips. I took a bite. "I will put a note on A Charming Cure telling them of your temporary location."

I chewed the egg roll and chewed on his idea. Which wasn't bad.

The businesses there were your typical flea market finds. Antique jewelry, pottery, children's clothes, children's toys. I couldn't forget the Indian family who sold all the Buddhist items. Darla had kept the rose Buddha in the kitchen window. His happy, laughing face had greeted her every morning and she loved it.

There was the Deep In the South booth where you could buy anything with the Kentucky stamp on it. The big belt buckles in these parts were a symbol of pride worn by most men. After they purchased their belt buckles, they could slide on over to the knife booth.

There was every type of knife anyone needed plus the accessories.

It was true that all men, other than Oscar, carried a knife attached to their belts. The knife booth was the place to go. The cell phone booth was on the rise when I left the flea market. I was sure it was booming now. I sighed happily. It was familiar and it was after all, home.

"I will support you with money. I'm just worried about you keeping yourself busy and not snooping around the investigation." His eyes warned me.

"You know me all too well." I put my container of vegetable fried rice on the bedside table next to me.

He put the flattened sack on the bedside table closest to him.

"Mmm." He pulled me back in his arms. "Let me show you how much I know you."

And I let him.

Chapter Fourteen

No, no. The sweat dripped down my face. The heat was what I imagined hell to be. I was stuck in hell. I waved my hands in front of me, fanning the smoke. Cough, cough. There had to be a way out. Out of the corner of my eye, Mr. Prince Charming's tail swayed in the smoke. Madame Torres was in his mouth. Yes! Yes! I'm coming! I tried to yell, but there was tape across my mouth. I lifted my hand to rip the tape off, but it wouldn't. I took my fingernail to peel the edges back. Nothing. I'm coming, my eyes screamed. The sweat had turned to salty tears. The smoke filled my lungs. I dropped. My hand landed on something. I pulled the object to me. A June's Gem?

Meow, meow. Mr. Prince Charming smacked his paws around on my face, waking me up from the nightmare I couldn't seem to get out of.

Gasp, gasp. I sat straight up in the bed, remembering where I was.

Locust Grove.

I patted my hand next to me. Oscar must've gone to work. The bed was empty and the clock read it was morning and time to get up. And the sunlight dotted through the window blinds.

Mewl. Mr. Prince Charming stood on the edge of my bed looking at me before he turned away and darted out my bedroom door.

I lay back on my pillow and stared at the faded glow-in-the-dark star stickers Darla had put on my ceiling.

"This will help your nightmares." Darla stepped up on the stepstool and peeled each star one-by-one placing them in smiling faces and in different shapes. After the stars were up, she turned out the light. The ceiling lit up like the night sky, only brighter. "And this." She pulled out her bottle of sleeping potion and shook it around my bed telling me the dream fairies would send me to dreamland and not nightmare land. And I believed her. Although the nightmares had never gone away.

"Oh, Darla." I groaned and rolled over to my side. The pain of the dream and the realization of a lost mother were almost too much for me to bare.

A tear trickled down my cheek. Something had to give.

Madame Torres glowed. The words were coming fast and furious. *Time, space, love, genes, DNA.*

Madame Torres was right. Taking pity on myself was not going to get me anywhere. I had my mother in my heart and in my head. Darla wouldn't want me to take pity. She'd force me to move forward. It was time I picked up and tried to move forward. Mac and Oscar would let me know what was going on.

I threw the sheets back and pulled on a pair of sweats and a tee before shuffling down the hall. The smell of fresh coffee drifted down the hall, leading me to the kitchen where Oscar had a pot of wake me up juice ready for me.

"This is exactly what I need." I opened the cabinet door and the coffee mugs were exactly where I had always kept them.

I pulled out Darla's Ghost Buster's mug, deciding to pour my cup. I picked up the Magical Cures Book she had also left me and took it over to the table. Carefully I sat it down on the table along with my mug and plopped down on the chair.

I ran my hand over the leather-bound book. I smiled remembering how I initially thought it was Darla's recipes for her homeopathic cures. Little did I realize it held a lot of secrets she couldn't open because she wasn't a spiritualist. In actuality, the book was handed down to me from my father's side of the family and Darla kept it safe.

Slowly I opened it, careful not to rip the binding and ran my hand over margins of the pages where Darla's handwriting had left notes. Notes that were meant for me and now I was able to interpret her instructions.

Like magic, my fingers tingled flowing into my blood. My gut knew what I had to do. Reopen the flea market shop. Just because I couldn't work in my shop in Whispering Falls, didn't mean I couldn't make my cures here. Oscar was right.

With my coffee in hand and Mr. Prince Charming at my feet, we headed out the back door and wandered over to the barely there shed.

"What can we do with this?" I asked Mr. Prince Charming and brushed my bed head hair out of my face.

Rowl. Mr. Prince Charming darted through the blown-off door and into the ruins. I didn't stop him because I figured he knew what he was doing.

Meow, meow. He appeared at the threshold, looked me in the eye and waved his tail.

I followed him in; surprised some of the things were still intact. The cabinets where my herbs from the herb garden were stored was untouched and there were beakers and burners under there too. I looked up. Most of the glass ceiling was gone, shattered from the explosion. The water the fire department had used to put out the burning shed had long been dried up leaving a lot of the stuff on the counter molded and brittle.

There was no time to think about what I was going to do, my intuition kicked in gear and I grabbed the trashcan on the side of the house, dragging it back to the shed. I found a pair of old winter gloves in one of the closets inside the house and an old broom. I was armed to clear out the shed and keep going with my life.

"I see you just can't stay out of trouble." The voice startled me when I was picking up a large piece of glass.

Luckily I didn't hurl the sharp object at my aunt when I twirled around.

"You scared the crap out of me." I held my hand up to my heart.

Aunt Helena Heal stood outside the shed, her long fingers wrapped around the shaft of a broom. She wore her head-to-toe signature black cloak and long dress. The tip of her black, heeled laced-up boots poked out from underneath the frock.

Rowl! Mr. Prince Charming darted past her; she swept the broom after him, teasing him even more.

Their fondness for each other was nowhere near fond.

"I still protest how he is your familiar," she growled, planting the bristles of the broom on the ground.

"He is, so get used to it." I rolled my eyes and went back to what I was doing. The last headache I wanted was for my only living relative to get on me for letting my shop burn to the ground and burning up a person.

Burning? Images of A Charming Cure swirled in my head. Was Gwendolyn burned? She had to have some burns if she was in the attic because it was charred. I tucked the question in the back of my head. Maybe the Karima sisters had their autopsy report and are able to answer my question.

I sucked in a deep breath.

"Your new mode of transportation?" I referred to her broom and threw a few more pieces of trash in the can.

Her cheeks darkened when her eyes squinted, causing her lashes to draw down.

"My, my." She drummed her long red nails together. "Aren't we ungrateful for the visit?"

"I'm sorry." I brushed my hair behind my ear with the back of my hand. I took the gloves off and sat them on the counter. "I'm a little stressed in case you hadn't heard the news."

"Oh I heard." She stepped inside the shed, looking around at the scope of the damage. "Why else do you think I'd risk leaving our safe spiritual world to come here?"

She was right. She never left the confines of the world in which we were safe. Our laws were different than the mortal world, our powers were lessoned when not in our world, and it was hard to blend in with the mortal world.

It was easy for me only because I was raised in the mortal world, but not Aunt Helena. She definitely would stick out like a sore thumb.

She picked up a piece of glass and threw it in the trashcan. "I know you had nothing to do with the burning shop." Her eyes popped open. Her nails dug into my palm when she grabbed my hand. "Why didn't you come to me?"

I drew my hand back. Wincing from the scrap of her nails.

"I. . ."I gulped. It had been a few months since I'd seen her.

She was the dean at Hidden Halls, A Spiritualist University. The only way to see her was to go through the portal in the middle of the woods beyond Eloise Sandlewood's tree house.

"I know I should have come to see you." As much as we bantered back and forth, I loved my aunt. She'd really been there for me since I found out about my gifts. In fact, I had studied under her when I moved to Whispering Falls; that seemed like a lifetime ago. Plus I did love the fact I had a blood relative on my side.

"Colton and Mac didn't give me much of a chance to gather my things before the lynching mob came after me." I shrugged remembering seeing Petunia lead the group up the hill toward my cottage.

"You have to go back." Helena glared at me. "You have to save Whispering Falls from evil."

"You are crazy if you think I'm doing that," I scoffed. There was no way on earth I would head back there.

"I'm not kidding. It's written in the stars." Aunt Helena wasn't taking no for an answer. "You're still the chosen one."

"Why would I go back?" I put the gloves back on and began to pick up more trash. This place wasn't going to clean itself and there was no secret potion to help me get it done. "I'm not the chosen one. Petunia is."

"You have to give up control as Village President or you will be banished if the Elders are called in." Her words stung me. "After you give up your presidency, things will fall in line."

"You mean they can't just hand over the gig to Petunia?" It seemed reasonable to me.

"You are the chosen one," she repeated.

"Not if I give up the presidency." I gulped.

"The chosen one doesn't mean you are president, June." Her voiced boomed, giving the ground a little shake. My eyes popped open. I felt like I was being scolded. "I'm not comfortable talking out here." She stepped back out of the shed, regaining her composure. "Do you have more coffee?"

"Yeah." The thought of going back to Whispering Falls while under suspicion that I killed someone didn't sit well. I peeled off the gloves and threw them on the counter. "Let's go in."

In silence, Aunt Helena followed Mr. Prince Charming and me in the back door.

"Charming." Aunt Helena glanced around. She leaned her broom up against the jamb of the door. "You know, Darla never invited me here once she moved you out of Whispering Falls."

"According to Eloise, it was for my protection." I took out another mug and filled both of ours. "Besides, I had a great childhood."

It was true; there wasn't anything I would change.

"I guess I could've stayed in touch but it was almost too much to bear." She lifted her hand to my face and gently rubbed down my cheek. "The thought of my brother's child being fatherless was almost too much for me. That was when I threw myself into my job and started to climb the administrative ladder."

"It all worked out." I sighed deeply, putting the hurt of the death of both my parents in the back of my thoughts. "Tell me this plan of yours."

"At midnight, I want you to slip in the cellar of Mystic Lights. There the village council, minus Petunia, will be waiting for you with the release ceremony." She lifted the mug, the steam floated around her head. She took a sip. "Then you will come back here and wait for the trial."

"Trial?" I gasped.

"I assume the autopsy report will show some sort of poison because I heard you had poison in the cauldron along with the remains of the IBS potion you had created." Aunt Helena shook her head. Her voice held disgust, "You have got to learn not everyone is going to like you. You hold the power and it shows whether you like it or not."

"I don't hold all this power." I didn't want to hear her words. They only frightened me. "I only wanted Gwendolyn to like me."

"Too late now. Remember my words, not everyone is going to like you. You hold too much power." Aunt Helena's words weren't making me feel better. She got to her feet. "It's time for me to get back."

She hugged me before she grabbed her broom. With her free hand, she flung her cloak around her disappearing into a flume of orange smoke. That was power. The kind of power I wanted. Not this child's play intuition.

To keep myself busy, I decided to go back outside and get my head wrapped around a plan to get some potions made so I could go back to the flea market and make a living until this nightmare was over with.

"Are you coming?" I opened the door and looked at Mr. Prince Charming who was on top of the kitchen counter staring out the window.

He didn't budge so I went outside without him.

"What the heck?" My jaw dropped at the sight of my shed.

The entire thing was back together as though the explosion never happened. The walls were there, the glass ceiling was not shattered, and the door was hung. Carefully I opened the door and peeked in before I dared step in.

The counter was in place. The beakers and burners were in place and plugged in. All the ingredients were in the spice rack I had used to keep them sorted was in place. The sink was there. Everything was there.

"You're welcome," Aunt Helena's voice whispered into the air.

I smiled.

Chapter Fifteen

The day was spent making new cures, keeping me happily busy, forgetting about the evil waiting for me in Whispering Falls.

"A dash of skullcap and a pinch of ginger." My hands moved around the shelves in front of me, tossing stuff in the boiler as though I hadn't missed a beat in my little shed. Neither time nor space could keep me from my gift. "There." I grabbed the wooden spoon and stirred the mix.

It was the perfect combination for someone with stress issues over money. Unfortunately, money was a big part of Locust Grove residents' stress problems. Whenever I was at the flea market, people would complain of stomachaches, acid reflux, headaches—all classic symptoms of stress. I would use my gift to hone in on their real underlying issues, which was mostly money.

"Aww." I grabbed a few of the old bottles under the cabinet I had collected from garage sales when growing up and picked out a couple to put the potion in.

The bottles weren't as pretty as the ones I used in A Charming Cure, but it would do for the flea market. Nor did they light up when I touched them. But I knew it was fine.

"I see you got a lot done today." Oscar was at the door. "You are so wrapped up, you didn't even notice that I've been standing here for about ten minutes."

"Yes!" I quickly poured the beakers into the bottles and corked them up. Using a sharpie marker, I wrote on the bottle. "Herbal Remedy: Antacid."

I held it out and looked at the first batch I was going to take to the flea market. I could feel some sort of pride coming back, filling my spirit.

"Aunt Helena came by to visit." I stopped myself. I kept the little secret about the meeting at midnight to myself. Oscar didn't need to know or he would discourage me from going. "She gave me a little pep talk and a present." I twirled around before I landed in Oscar's arms.

"I couldn't wait until I got home to see you." He buried his head into my neck. "I thought we could head out to grab a bite to eat. Like a date."

"Sounds perfect. All of this work has got me hungry." I couldn't remember the last time I had actually eaten. Another thing Oscar didn't need to know, or he would be hovering over me. I didn't need a babysitter. "I'll go get ready."

"I'll get changed." He pointed to his cruiser. "I got a change of clothes in the car."

He headed one way and I headed the other. It was odd how he didn't mention anything about the fire or Gwendolyn's murder. Maybe he was going to give me some information at dinner. Or maybe he was going to let me enjoy a night out, putting the stress aside for a few moments. The only time I didn't seem to be stressed was when I was lost in my potions.

I hurried in and grabbed an orange dress. Oscar always said I looked good in orange. I strapped on some black heels and ran a comb through my bob.

"Are you ready?" I asked Oscar.

He sat in the family room with a cute teal button down and dark jeans on. He had the sleeves rolled up to three-quarters length. He had the perfect amount of gel in his black hair. He looked adorable.

"You look beautiful." His eyes danced. He looked lovingly at me. "I'm so lucky. Smart, beautiful and sexy."

He reached out and I grabbed his hand. He lifted my hand to his lips and kissed my mother's ring he'd used to propose to me.

"I'm the lucky one." I laughed. "Do you remember when I sabotaged your date with what's-her-name?"

"Let's not bring that up." He brought me in for a kiss to shut me up.

I giggled remembering the little spell I'd put on a date he had a year ago. That was when I knew I'd fallen—hook, line, and sinker—for him and there was no one going to get in my way.

Instead of taking his cruiser, I let him take the Green Machine. Something about being in a cop car wasn't appealing to me. I didn't want to tempt fate and see into the future. Because that was where I was going to be transported if we didn't figure out what happened to Gwendolyn.

We settled on a little Indian place in the strip mall in Locust Grove. Once inside, you were transported into what I could only imagine an authentic restaurant would look like in India. The tables were low to the ground; large pillows on the floor was where everyone was seated.

After placing our order, I knew I couldn't dance around the big elephant in the room.

"Did you find out if the autopsy is back yet?" I asked.

"Not yet." Oscar shook his head. "Colton said any day. But he did tell me there was a match found in the attic along with a trail of some sort of mixture."

"Like gasoline?" I asked.

"I guess." He pinched his lips. "Colton isn't letting me get in on the evidence at all. I guess it's best so

Petunia and her family can't claim I'm leaving out details because you are engaged to me."

"You know, I'm not the only one who had words with Gwenie." I hated to rat people out, but I wasn't going to be the only one with the pointing finger.

Oscar jabbed at his plate of Chicken Shahi Korma.

"Izzy and Raven had words with Gwenie. Not only did she put my shop down, she put theirs down as well. She told Raven her tarts were tart, not good. And she said Izzy's shop wasn't run right. So why aren't they being investigated?"

"Maybe they are. Colton isn't telling me anything." Oscar's brows furrowed. "I'm sure he's on top of it. But you also have to look at the fact that she wasn't found dead in their shops. She was found dead in yours."

"Thanks for reminding me." I forked a piece of his chicken off his plate. "Chandra mentioned something to me about how everyone said Gwenie was being nasty to everyone."

"I need to tell Colton this." Oscar tapped his fork on his plate. "Are you sure?"

"Positive."

"And I'm not so sure Petunia has forgiven me for stepping on her toes and taking the presidency when I moved there because her family and her friend have all mentioned it to me."

"I don't think Petunia is the killer if that is what you are thinking." Oscar stared at me.

"Who said Gwenie was murdered?" I gulped. "What if she was trying to get back at me for hurting Petunia in the past? I didn't lock the door behind me that night. She probably knew it and slipped back in."

"What?" Oscar shook his head. "Tell me word for word what happened."

"After I made the IBS remedy for her, which had no potion in it. Strictly herbal." It was important I was clear about no potion so he would know I didn't put anything funny in my cauldron. "She told me she was going back to Glorybee. I went back up to the ceremony and she never showed up. I bet she waited for me to start the ceremony and she went back in the shop. Did her little voodoo or whatever she did and set the place on fire.

Only," I paused, "she didn't get out in time and her plan backfired. Literally."

"Not bad." Oscar's eyes squinted. He had a faraway look. "Not bad, June Heal. Maybe you should be wearing the badge, not me." He smiled, sending my heart into all sorts of spirals.

"I'm just trying to look at it from all angles."

"Or you could've been framed." His head tilted to the side.

"Which brings me to another conclusion." I took a bite of food.

"I don't like the sound of that."

"Let's say someone was trying to frame me. They knew I was talking to Gwenie in my shop. They saw us go in or something." I didn't know what the something was, so I just went with it. "When we left, they saw I didn't lock the door. They killed Gwenie, dragged her into my shop and set it on fire. Only they wanted to catch her body on fire, trying to disguise how she was really killed. The fire was put out before her body got burned."

"She wasn't burned." Oscar's jaw dropped when the realization that her body was perfectly intact and burn free. "She wasn't burned at all."

"Right." I gulped. "Which means someone really is trying to frame me." My heart beat rapidly, my palms were sweating. Suddenly I wasn't so hungry anymore. "But who?"

Chapter Sixteen

Oscar was too excited with the sleuthing we had concocted at dinner to stay over. He said he was going to go back to Whispering Falls and run it all by Colton. I encouraged him to stay the night there at his place since it would be too late to drive back, not to mention I had to go to Mystic Lights without him knowing.

"Are you sure?" he asked standing under the porch light of my house. "I don't know."

"I'm going to be fine." I pointed down at Mr. Prince Charming, who was batting around a few cicadas on the step before flicking them off onto the ground into the cicada cemetery with all the other victims who fell prey to him.

Oscar ran his fingers down the side of my face, tracing my lips with his finger.

"I swear to God." He rested his palm on my cheek. "If I find out someone is trying to frame you, they will have to deal with me."

"It's all going to be fine." I tried to keep my voice steady when the images of the latest nightmare shook my memory.

Unfortunately, my intuition told me it was going to get much worse before it was going to get better.

I rolled up on my toes, wrapped my hand around his neck, bringing his lips to mine. I was shocked at how eager I was to kiss him.

"Are you sure you don't want me to drive back?" he whispered, his breath hot against my lips. "There will be more of this."

There we stood. On the porch of my childhood home making out like a couple of horny teenagers.

Ahem, someone clearing his throat made me pull away, but Oscar continued to try to kiss me.

"Oscar." I poked Oscar in the chest, and then slid my finger over to Mac McGurtle.

"I get it. I get it." Oscar put his hands in the air like he was surrendering. "Mac, I'm expecting you to take care of my gal."

"I'll do my best." Mac cleared his throat and waited for Oscar to make his exit.

"Tell Mac what you told me." Oscar pointed to me. A stern look on his face. "I'll let you know about that body."

I waved Oscar off and waved Mac in. Mr. Prince Charming took his spot on the radiator. When Mac passed, he gave Mr. Prince Charming a good scratch.

Purr, purrrr. Mr. Prince Charming had a smile on his face.

"Let's get down to business, shall we." Mac used the briefcase in his hand to point in the direction of the couch in the family room.

When I followed him in there, it hit me that there weren't any family pictures in my house. The only picture I had of me and Darla was hanging on the wall in A Charming Cure.

"Are you okay?" Mac asked.

I bit my lip and nodded my head. I wasn't. I had to get that picture. Tonight.

Mac smacked his briefcase down on the coffee table, catching my attention. He rolled the fancy lock with his thick fingers and slid them open. He pushed his glasses up on the bridge of his nose before he opened the briefcase. He took out a file folder with Gwenie's name across it.

"The autopsy is not back yet." He looked at me over the rims of his glasses. "At least that is what I could get out of Patience. Not that she is much help, but I gave her some lettuce for her ostrich."

Patience would do anything for her pet ostrich. I couldn't say that for the feathery bird. Every time I saw them, he looked like he was trying to get away from her.

"Good move." I smiled, knowing how happy that probably made Patience.

"Anyway." He lifted his hands. "They are hoping to have it complete in the next two days. Something about the family wanting them to send off the samples to their village in Florida."

"Understandable." Some relief sat in my gut. At least it gave me a couple days minimum to figure it all out.

"The samples are all taken and sent off, which means the body is ready for burial." He opened the file. "The family is going to hold a service for them at Two Sisters tomorrow and tonight the sisters are going to cremate her."

"Cremate?" I asked. It was unusual for a family to have a cremation without some sort of ceremony.

"Yeah, around midnight or something strange like that." He shrugged. "Each village is different."

I was going to have to get around Whispering Falls without anyone seeing me. Evidently there was a lot going to be happening around midnight.

"Full moon!" I smacked my leg, which hurt since my dress didn't cover all my thighs.

"Excuse me?"

"Nothing." I played it off, but during a full moon, cremation was big. It was said the spirits of evil were kept at bay from the glow of the full moon, leaving only loving spirits. This made sure the deceased person being cremated wasn't brought back as someone's familiar or as an animal, like the fireflies.

Since Petunia was an animal reader, most of her clients lived past lives as spiritualists. They would make sure Gwenie moved on. That had to be it, I just knew it. Regardless, I was going to steer way clear from them and Two Sisters and a Funeral.

"What did Oscar want you to tell me?" Mac grabbed a pen and paper. I told him my two theories. He agreed it could be plausible and he'd use his resources to check into it.

Unfortunately, his timing wasn't as quick as my timing. I would be one step ahead of him and anyone else Oscar decided to tell.

When Mac left, I changed my dress into a pair of jeans and comfy sweatshirt. I had a couple hours to kill. I didn't want to wait around, so I decided to make a quick house call to Adeline.

"You stay here." I instructed Mr. Prince Charming.

He darted in between and around my legs in
protest. I bent down to pick him up and he swatted at
my wrist.

"Ouch!" I grabbed my wrist, realizing he only
wanted me to wear my charm bracelet. "Fine. Fine. But
you don't have to be a jerk."

Rowl! He darted off underneath my bed.

Madame Torres lit up next to the bed. The hot pink
words glowed in the depths of her black ball. *Anger,
bitter, annoyed, death.*

"I'll be fine," I said one more time. I wasn't sure
whom I was trying to convince. Mr. Prince Charming,
Madame Torres, or me.

I drove the Green Machine down Adeline's street. It
was the typical neighborhood in Locust Grove. The
houses were all cape cod style, but Adeline had the best
yard in her subdivision. Her flowerbed running along the
front of the house was neatly kept and the yard was
perfectly manicured. Adeline's car was in the driveway.

I pulled behind hers.

The porch light flipped on when I knocked on her door.

"June," Adeline's voice escalated. She pulled the door wide open. Her small frame stood there in her pajamas. She tucked a strand of her sandy blond hair behind her ear. "What are you doing in Locust Grove?"

"I'm staying at my old house for a while, so I thought I'd stop by for a quick hello." I didn't technically lie. I just didn't tell her I was a number one suspect for murder.

"Come in if you don't mind me in my pj's." She stepped aside, making enough room for me to come in.

"Of course I don't." I stepped into the grey foyer. I loved how she decorated with black hardwood floors and the wainscoting on the bottom half of the wall. A delicate crystal chandelier hung from the center of the ceiling making her romantic shabby chic style of decorating stand out.

"Don't mind my house. It's a little messy." Adeline used her good southern charm when we both knew there was no mess.

"Can I get you something to drink?" she asked.

"No, don't make a fuss. I wanted to get a schedule of your yoga classes." It sounded like a good idea. If I was going to be in Locust Grove, I might as well hang out with my friend. . .until they came for me with the paddy wagon.

"I have a schedule in here." She motioned me to follow her into her kitchen.

Her style of decorating ran flawlessly throughout the house. She plucked something out of a cute wire rack that was nailed on the side of one of the whitewashed kitchen cabinets. She handed me piece of paper. It was a schedule from the YMCA and her classes were circled in pink.

She leaned on the butcher-block island, using her elbows to prop herself up. She looked at me. "I'd love to have you. Tomorrow night will be perfect."

"It just might work." I tapped the paper. "I'm going to go to the flea market tomorrow to get an application to open a booth."

"You are?" She drew back.

"Why not?"

"Okay..." Nervously, she walked over to the window and started to adjust the lace curtains in the window. "Not that you would tell me or anything, but what about your shop?"

"My shop." I let out a heavy sigh. "There was a fire and I can't work there until after the fire marshal finishes up the investigation report."

"Fire?" Adeline's mouth formed in disbelief. "Really?"

"Yeah." I shook my head. There was no way I could tell her the truth. She already had her suspicions about the real magic happening around Whispering Falls. She didn't have it all figured out but she was close. "It happened at night. I guess I forgot to turn off my cauld. . ." I stopped myself. "My stove where I make my herbs."

"That is awful." Sadness appeared in her eyes. "What are you going to do?"

"For now I need to keep busy and make a living until the investigation is over so I'm going to stay in my home here and work at the flea market." I smiled. "You never know, I just might have two A Charming Cure locations.

One here and one in Whispering Falls."

"Look at you going big." She grinned ear to ear.

Chapter Seventeen

My visit with Adeline was exactly what I needed. A little girl time without all the talk about burning buildings and dead bodies. I told her to expect me at the yoga class. It was going to be a good relief after what I thought was going to be a long day. And she said she'd help me set up my booth in the morning.

The back roads to Whispering Falls were dark. I'd rely on my intuition to get into the village.

I stopped the Green Machine on the edge of town and read the old beat-up wooden sign, "Welcome to Whispering Falls, A Charming Village."

I turned the lights off on the car and tapped the wheel.

"Charming alright," I groaned, trying to decide my next move.

The lynching mob wouldn't be around because according to Mac, they were all going to be at Two Sisters and a Funeral for the cremation of Gwenie. It wasn't like I could roll the car through town and up to my cottage because they would see me.

This was the moment I wished I had Aunt Helena's broom or even the gift to drive the darn thing. Instead, I had to pull the El Camino in a wooded area off the side of the road and hoof it through the woods into town.

Two Sisters was the first business into town and I made sure I wasn't seen. I kept hidden in the deep shadows of the trees, even with the moonbeams beating down. The sounds of chains and chants caught my attention.

I tiptoed from behind, tree-to-tree, getting closer and closer to the singing. In the distance, Eloise swung the ball of incense down Main Street.

"Incense, sweet and fine, cleanse this area of mine. Purge this place of magical space. Mother Earth cleanse us free for this is the space we want you to be. Hands to the sky and hearts to the heavens, make us whole an even leaven." Eloise swung the chain up and down each side of her body. The smell of cinnamon filled the air with each puff of smoke.

The lights of Two Sisters were on. Through the windows, I could see shadows moving about.

"It's about time you got here." Eloise stood next to me.

"You scared me." I jumped around, breaking a few branches beneath me. My hot breath caught the nip of the night air. "I guess I should've known you saw me."

"The incense lets me see your aura over here hiding and rightfully so." She swung the incense around me. "It couldn't hurt to cleanse you too." She winked.

"Ya think?" Sarcasm dripped in my tone.

"Oscar did give me a hint about what has been going on. He said you were going to reopen your flea market shop," she said.

Her eyes held the sympathy gaze I hated. I didn't want people feeling sorry for me.

"It doesn't sound good." She rubbed her hand down my arm. "Do you want to talk about it?"

"I would love to, but I'm not supposed to be in town." I was probably wasting my breath because I bet she already knew that. "I'm on my way to officially resign my position as Village President."

A faint light came from the inside of Mystic Lights and it was my cue to get over there.

"You know I will be more than willing to help you if you need me." She said her words as if she had a deeper meaning but I didn't have time to question her.

"I appreciate that." I turned back to Eloise, but she was gone as quick as she had appeared.

The nighttime wind whipped and howled around me. The moon was still full and a low cloud hung around creating enough shadow for me to slip past the side windows of Two Sisters.

Petunia, Peony, and Amethyst were talking to Constance. By the looks of it, Constance was holding a file. Unfortunately, I couldn't see what was on it, other than a doodle or two, which was probably made by Patience because she was sitting at the table doodling on something while the other four huddled.

What I wouldn't give to get my hands on the file. Inwardly, I groaned and moved with the moon's shadow as the cloud moved along the surface, leading me to the back of Mystic Lights. The cellar door was propped open, which was my invitation to go on in.

Before I slipped down the stairs, my intuition told me to look around. I took a quick glance into the black night. Everything was still and just as it should be. The faint light coming from the guts of Mystic Lights was made by a few candles with Gerald, Izzy, and Chandra gathered around.

"I'm glad you made it safely," Izzy said and wasted no time drawing the ceremonial book up to the candle's wick. Gerald and Chandra didn't look at me. Their hands folded in front of them. Silent.

"Seriously?" I questioned, breaking the silence between us. "You can't possibly think I had anything to do with Gwenie's death?"

"Please get on with this. Petunia is already upset that her husband has to make a special tea as they are having a private family ceremony at Two Sisters." Gerald kept his head down, talking about himself in third person.

"Gerald." I had to get him to look at me. "I did not set my own building on fire. At least believe that."

"Oh, honey." Chandra reached out and touched me. "We know you wouldn't hurt a flea while in your right mind and we also know you love your shop."

"What does that mean?" I drew back, ignoring the comment on how I love my shop. More disturbing was the in my right mind comment. "I am in my right mind."

"I think what she is saying is that you weren't raised a spiritualist and sometimes we see those types use their gifts for evil." Izzy did a poor job of reading Chandra's words because it set me on fire. "I think we can all agree something evil is lingering in the air and the only way to get things done while you are in Locust Grove is to give Petunia the presidency she was going to get before all of this happened."

"I'm glad you feel the evil too because that is what is behind the fire and Gwenie's death. I just know it, but as far as me not being raised as a spiritualist. . ." I put my hand on my chest and sucked in a deep breath. "You are the one who dragged me here and I'm a Good-Sider."

Good-sider!

I gasped, trying to get in some air when my intuition socked the breath right out of me. Spiritualists are classified into two categories. The Good-Siders and the Dark-Siders. It was a hard concept for me as a spiritualist to segregate the two so I had proposed a new law to include everyone and it had passed. Whispering Falls became a community for all.

In the old days, Dark-Siders were more on the darker side of magic. A dash of spells with a little kick to it. While the Good-Siders only used goodness for magic. Eloise and Raven were perfect examples of good Dark-Siders.

But what took my breath away was the Full Moon Treesort. Was Amethyst a Dark-Sider? Was that why she had to put her shop in the forest? That was why Eloise lived in the woods. Was it the same for Amethyst? Did she have something against Gwendolyn? Did she have something against me?

These were all valid questions to explore and I knew the only way I was going to get answers was to snoop around Full Moon. Maybe I would take Eloise up on her offer to come visit. Not tonight. Maybe tomorrow.

"Did you hear me, June?" Izzy's voice boomed in the under girth of the building. "I asked, are you freely giving up your duties as Village President and passing them along to Petunia Shrubwood?"

"Yes," I stated.

Izzy raised her hands to her mouth. She licked her finger and thumb before she used them to smoother the light of the wick. Her eyes turned to me. They lowered, putting a chill into an already chilly cellar.

"You may excuse yourself now." Izzy's finger thrust toward the cellar steps.

I bit back tears and bitter words and went as I was instructed. At the top of the steps, there was a pink and green box. I looked over at the backside of Wicked Good Bakery where the lights were on. It wasn't unusual for Raven to be in there baking and doing her thing, getting ready for the morning rush.

Quickly I picked it up. She had obviously seen me duck into the cellar and it was just like her to leave a treat for me when I was stressed. I'm sure she saw it in the dough.

Goosebumps traveled up my legs and trickling up my arms, telling me it was time to get out of Whispering Falls. With the box tucked under my arm, I followed the shadow of the cloud only it didn't take me to the Green Machine. It took me to the steps of A Charming Cure.

Chapter Eighteen

"No. I shouldn't," I whispered while biting the inside of my lip. "Oh, but I should."

I didn't let anything hold me back. I tiptoed up the steps and turned the knob. I was happy to see it was locked, so I pulled my set of keys out of my pocket and unlocked it, slipping in.

Even with the smell of burnt wood, the smell of the shop came flooding back. My heart fell to my feet. The realization of Gwendolyn's death set in. Someone had come into my shop and used it to plan out their crime.

Who would do such a thing? The question rolled in my thoughts. Before I walked toward the back to where the pull-down attic stairs were, I plucked my picture of me and my parents off the wall and held it tight to my chest. It was the only picture I had of us and there was no way I was going to leave here without it.

Along with the picture, I grabbed a bag from behind the counter and ran my hands down the ingredients bookshelf. Every bottle that lit up, I placed in the bag. There was no use in leaving them. I could definitely use them at the flea market booth. And something told me I might need them to help solve the case. But how?

I would not try to figure it out. My intuition would tell me when it was time.

"I suggest you get out of here." Eloise appeared inside of the shop. She stood next to the front window with her finger pulling back the curtain. She bobbled her head back and forth looking out into the street. "I think someone knows you are in here because Colton and Petunia are crossing the street."

"Crap." I held the bag and picture close to me. "How in the hell are we going to get out?"

"Well," Eloise sucked in like I was annoying her. "Help me." She rushed back to my storage room in the back of the shop where I kept a refrigerator and a small living room.

I'm guilty of taking naps during the day or even late at night while I was up making and creating new potions.

It was there when I took over the shop that it reminded me most of Darla.

I hurried behind Eloise. She stood next to the wooden table, which had never been moved. Underneath it was an old wool rug. It was definitely Darla's taste in using the natural elements to decorate.

"You get on that side." Eloise bent down and placed her hands under the table. "We will move the table over there." Her head nodded to the wall on the other side of the room.

I did what she said. The bell over the shop door dinged.

"Is anyone in here?" Colton called out, echoing into the storage room.

Eloise placed her finger over top her mouth, signaling me to not say a word. She flipped up the edge of the rug, uncovering a trap door. Slowly she pulled it up, exposing a set of stairs and some lights. With magic, she tapped the first candle and all of them lit up.

She pointed for me to go down there. I didn't protest. I went. I stopped a few steps down and looked up. She had pulled the edge of the carpet as good as she could so it would cover the door once she shut it behind her.

She shooed me with her hand to go once she had closed the trapdoor. I cleared thick cobwebs on my way down and stopped at the bottom. The candles lit up a long cobblestone hallway, giving me the creeps.

"Go on." Eloise put her hand on my back.

"Where does this go?" I questioned. "Wait! I forgot my June's Gems." I had set the box on the counter when I filled the bag with the herbs.

"Move. And forget the gems." Eloise pushed in front of me. "It is how Darla and I use to hang out when she lived here."

"Really?" I stayed on Eloise's heels and continually looked back. As we walked, the candles behind us burned out.

"In case you forgot, I'm a Dark-Sider and I wasn't too welcome in the community. Since Darla and I were best friends, and she needed my magic for the shop, I magically made a tunnel for us to go from her shop to the tree house." Eloise's cloak swished with each turn and curve as we made our way closer and closer to her house. "It was a lot of fun too. You know." Eloise stopped and turned to me. "She would be so proud of you. And she would have loved to show you this tunnel." She reached down and grabbed my hand, rubbing her finger over my engagement ring. "Every time I look at your hand, I see hers."

"I'm so grateful I have you to tell me about Darla." I gave a half smile. The best I could muster up since I was currently in a stressful situation. "I really do wish I remembered when we lived here."

"You were just a baby." She turned and headed on down the corridor without looking back until we made it to another set of steps leading up to a door.

Eloise used the flat of her hand and pushed the door up over her head. Light pierced the dark steps from above. I squinted, trying to let my eyes adjust to the darkness. One by one, I planted one foot on a step and then the other, doing it all the way up into the green house of Eloise's garden.

"Shoo." Eloise ran her hands down the front of her cloak, brushing off the dust and cobwebs from the tunnel. "That was a close call."

She picked off different flowers, making her way to the door of the greenhouse. Before opening the door, she picked up the spray bottle and gave a couple sprits to a wilted-looking potted plant, springing it back to life in an instant.

"I really should come in here more often." A look of satisfaction was on her face. She put the bottle back in its place and opened the door.

We walked through the rows of her garden; the twinkling lights in the tree branches brought the happy, magical feeling back into my soul. These were the times I felt everything just might turn out okay.

The small wooden signs on the garden were painted with the names of the herbs: Rose petals, moonflower, mandrake root, seaweed, shrinking violet, dream dust, magic peanut, lucky clover, steal rose.

"Fairy dust." I bent down when my intuition stopped me in my tracks. "Do you mind if I pick a few because I want to put some in my dream potion."

"Of course." Eloise twirled her hand in the air and clapped twice.

Two one-inch purple fairies twisted and turned, gathering the dust on the plant. With their tiny hands, they blew, sending the dust up to me in little cubes. I picked the floating cubes out of the air and stuck them in my bag.

"Thank you." I had to stop the nightmares and I was willing to do anything to make it happen. Regardless, they did prepare me for the future and what might happen, but at this point, nothing could get worse.

Meow, mewl. Mr. Prince Charming darted around my ankles doing his signature figure eight.

"Now you come." My mouth twitched. He darted toward the gazebo in the garden where Eloise was seated at the small café table. She motioned me over.

"Let's have a midnight snack." The three-tiered stand held finger sandwiches and tarts. She picked up

the pink china teakettle and evenly poured the liquid
into a teacup in front of her and one in front of the
empty seat to which she gestured me to sit down.

I did, putting the picture frame of my family and the
bag of herbs on the ground. I kept my bag strapped
across my shoulder.

"So, tell me." Eloise pushed the food toward me.
She picked up a tart and popped it in her mouth. "Why
are you here when Oscar clearly told you to stay in
Locust Grove?"

"Yes. I told you to stay put." Oscar walked down the
lighted pathway from the front of the house. "I went
back to Locust Grove because I didn't want you to stay
there alone and the fact you insisted I stay in Whispering
Falls tonight did give me the idea you had something up
your sleeve. So I called Aunt Eloise and sent her to look
for you."

"Oh." I folded my hands in my lap. "I was
summonsed here by Aunt Helena to give up my
presidency in a ceremony in the cellar at Mystic Lights. I

wanted to get the picture of my family and bring it to Locust Grove. That was it."

Oscar's brows rose. "That is the only reason you went to your shop?"

"Fine." He wasn't buying it. I said, "When I made it into town, I couldn't help myself. I looked into Two Sisters where they were having the final cremation for Gwenie. Then I wanted to check out the shop for any evidence because I didn't do it."

"Let the law handle it." Oscar stepped up into the gazebo and stuffed a finger sandwich in his mouth.

"Plus I have my eyes and ears planted around the village." Eloise put a little ease to my fears knowing I had someone on the inside watching out for me.

Eloise and Oscar finished off the food. I pulled my cloak around me. The night air was getting colder. The sounds of the night engulfed me. They were much different at night then the day. I wasn't used to the crickets, the lightning bugs, croakers, and frogs, not to mention the bright yellow snake wrapped around the

wooden spindle of the gazebo. The beady eyes didn't
stop looking at me.

Chapter Nineteen

"Did you see that snake?" I asked Oscar the next day when we were having our coffee at the table back in Locust Grove. It was a great way to avoid talking about the night before and the situation I'd put him in since he was sheriff of Whispering Falls. "It was huge." I shimmied, thinking of the big slithery thing. "I'm so glad I don't have to stay up in the night for my gift."

"I didn't." Oscar dropped the corner of the paper. His big blue eyes looked at me. "But, you know, anything in Aunt Eloise's garden is not going to hurt you."

"I know." I picked up a couple of the bottles and placed them in the cardboard box I was going to use to take my cures to the flea market. "Still, I swear the thing was looking at me. Besides, I don't like snakes anyway."

"Is this your way of ignoring the fact you went against the law and making idle chit chat because you know you are putting me in a tough situation?" Oscar wasn't going to let last night's mess-up go away like I had hoped.

"No. But nothing happened. I did what I was told and now Petunia is the Village President." I adjusted a few of the bottles in the box to avoid eye contact. "And if I hadn't gone to your aunt's, I'd never gotten these little babies."

I picked up a couple cubes of the fairy dust.

"These are why I slept so good last night." I exhaled a happy sigh. "No nightmare."

"June Heal," Oscar folded the paper and laid it in front of him. "You make breaking the law a no big deal in your own cute way."

He reached out, dragging me into his lap, in a mini-make-out session until someone knocked on the door.

"Who is that?" His eyes slid toward the hallway. His brows furrowed.

"Ooh!" Excited I jumped up. "I forgot." I darted down the hallway, calling behind me, "I went to see Adeline last night and she's going to help me go to the flea market to set up my booth."

"Great." The sound in Oscar's voice wasn't so joyous. "You know she's a mortal right?"

"Of course, silly." I swung the door open. "Hi!"

"Good morning." She stuck her hand out with a coffee. "I figured you didn't do your morning yoga moves I showed you. Coffee is probably just as good for you." She winked handing me the cup. "Are you ready?"

"Yep." I held the door open for her. Mr. Prince Charming was on cue, darting across the radiator, his tail jutted out catching Adeline's attention, waiting for a good scratch.

"You are a good kitty. Yes you are." Adeline talked baby talk, turning Mr. Prince Charming off.

Growl! He hissed darting down the hall into the bedroom.

Adeline jumped back. "He's not very nice."

"He has his moments," I called over my shoulder and played with my charm bracelet. It was the first thing Oscar made me put on this morning when we got out of bed.

I bent down and kissed Oscar one more time, knowing I wasn't going to see him until later tonight after his shift at the station in Whispering Falls. "Have a good day. Find some evidence that isn't against me," I suggested in a half-joking manner.

I grabbed the box. Adeline got in her car and I got in the Green Machine. She followed me to the fairgrounds on the west side of Locust Grove where the flea market was set up.

Dust spun off the tires of our cars, creating a thin dirty layer on our windshields. The grass had already turned brown, waiting for Mother Nature and winter to set in. The dull weather made my soul hurt. Whispering Falls was always so colorful. Full of life. We told visitors it was due to being nestled in the mountainous regions of Kentucky when in actuality the magic flowed through the village, bringing everything full of life.

"It's busy." I noticed we had to park in the far lot of the fairgrounds.

Adeline had told me the flea market was now open seven days a week. Much different from the weekend only hours I was used to. The idea of me being busy in the shed and making new cures on a daily basis did help put the memories of the nightmares, and dead body, a little more at bay.

I grabbed the box, Adeline grabbed our coffees, and we headed in for the office to sign up. After a few signatures, everything was ready. They had even given me the same spot I had before moving to Whispering Falls.

"I'm going to grab another cup of coffee from the trailer over there while you start to unpack." Adeline pointed in the direction of the food trailers, which weren't there before. "Then you can tell me what goes where."

"Sounds good," I said.

I waited until she was out of sight and no one was looking to do my thing. I had made a special potion for this occasion. A "do it" potion where I had visualized what I wanted the booth to look like. I uncorked the top and sprinkled it around the base of the booth. Before I could even dash the last drop out, the booth had already been transformed.

The red shelves lined the two side walls and the back. All the glass bottles were arranged in categories like the shop. One side was homeopathic cures for things like stress, stomachaches, and gout. The back wall was remedies for ailments. And the other side wall was for women's creams for wrinkles, gooseneck, fingernails and any other beauty aid they might ask about.

The crystal chandelier hung in the middle had over fifty lit candles that were scented in the customer's favorite smell. Not everyone liked the smell of vanilla bean or pumpkin spice. Some people like chocolate chip cookie dough smell or even pine. So I made the candles a special scent to take on the favorite smell of anyone who walked into my booth, almost guaranteeing me a sale.

The large area rug in the center was tan and brought the gleaming bottles and soft candlelight together. If this didn't draw in the crowd at least out of curiosity, I had no other idea what would, because looking around was only the typical flea market booths. The people hung their wares from the clotheslines with pins and clips. There was junk strewn around on tables in no particular order. The only booth with somewhat a cohesive look was the belt buckle people with their glass cases sitting on top of the card tables.

"What in the hell?" Adeline nearly dropped the cups of coffee in her hands. "How did you get this done so fast?"

"I'm quick." I brushed my hands together and clicked the backs of my heels.

I had opted to wear a black A-line skirt and a magenta top. Oscar had always liked the way my dark eyes and hair light up when I had the top on. I was relying on his comments to have the same effect on my customers. I needed all the sales I could get. Not only to pay for my living expenses in Locust Grove, but also for any legal fees I would be incurring with Mac. Which made me wonder why I hadn't heard from him today.

I was expecting a call from him to make sure I had gone to the releasing ceremony last night. Maybe he was waiting to call when he had some solid leads on the case. I wanted to ask him about the autopsy.

"Quick isn't the word." Adeline's face contorted. She handed off my coffee and made a beeline to the women's facial creams. "I swear there is something new every time I turn around. Time In A Bottle?" She held it up to me.

"Darnelle, look!" A pudgy blond woman rushed toward me in a very colorful tie-dyed t-shirt making her look much larger than she already was. Her nose was pig-like and when she talked, her blue eyes squinted and her cheeks balled up. "It's that shop I've been looking for. And she has the facial cream now." The woman jerked the bottle out of Adeline's hands. "Last time I saw you, you said you didn't have facial cream."

The memory of her voice came back to me. Only she was much larger than the last time I had seen her. Her plump face was so full, there wasn't nearly a wrinkle that hadn't been stretched out.

"I'm back and I have been waiting to see you." I took a pink bottle off the wrinkle cream shelf. The one with the Belladonna root.

I had spent years trying to find the root and it was next to impossible. Luckily for me, Eloise grew a big bunch in her garden and she gave me all the supply I needed for the perfect solution for the ever-growing population of women around the world with crows feet nestling on their faces.

"This is exactly what you were looking for last time I was here." I displayed the bottle in the palm of my hand.

The woman shoved the other bottle back in Adeline's hands and grabbed the pink bottle out of my palm.

"Darnelle, I want every bottle she has here." She used the back of her hand to smack Darnelle in the arm. In her deep southern accent, she asked, "Did you hear me?" She berated poor ole Darnelle, who stood there like she had cut off his manhood. "I said," her lips thinned, her white teeth gritted, "Did. You. Hear. Me?" As though Darnelle was deaf.

"Yes, dear," Darnelle sounded defeated.

Dang, I was hoping against all hope, Darnelle was going to come back with a zinger, but he didn't. Darnelle patiently took the three bottles off the shelf and sat them on the counter.

"We will take all four." He pointed to the three and then the one in his wife's death grip. "What's this going to cost me?"

"Eighty dollars." I had figured she would pay anything for the creams, but twenty sounded like a good amount. Especially since she was buying me out.

"Eighty dollars?" Peony appeared from the next booth over. "It better be a miracle cream."

"Oh, honey." The lady held the bottle up to Peony's face. "It's all mine. Come on Darnelle." She fussed, opening the jar and sticking her finger in the cream, slathering it all over her face, but not before taking a few of my business cards and stuffing them in her bra.

"Peony," I welcomed her. "How did you know where I was?"

I was happy to see someone from home. Not that the flea market wasn't home, but home was where my joy was. Right now I wanted everything to be as normal as it was two days ago.

"Adeline." She pointed to Adeline.

"Guilty!" She put her hand in the air. "When I came to your shop the other day, Peony heard us talking about yoga. She's an avid practitioner."

"You are?" I asked. No wonder her body was so lean. I pegged it to be her age, making me feel better about my own self.

"I am." Peony picked up a bottle here and there looking at the words printed on the glass. "I went to a class this morning and she said she was helping you open your flea market booth back up."

"You had a class this morning?" I questioned. "I thought it was tonight?"

"It's for all those people who love to do sunrise yoga." Her smile grew as the deep breath she sucked in filled her lungs. "I'm still having tonight."

"The sunrise is exactly what our people would love." Peony smiled and twisted side to side. "I could totally open a yoga studio in Whispering Falls."

My eyes grew and my face stilled. Peony had to stop throwing around comments about the spiritual community like everyone in the world knew about us.

"Our people?" Adeline looked between Peony and me.

"Yoga lovers. Isn't that right?" I looked at Peony, giving her the stink eye.

"Yes. Yep." She bounced on the pad of her high heels. "Yoga lovers." She snapped her fingers in the air. "Yoginis."

"You know." I switched the subject. Quickly. "I'm going to be busy tonight working on new creams."

"That will keep you busy." Peony continued to look around, not getting the hint of keeping her trap shut.

My cup of coffee was on the edge of the card table the flea market provided for the booths. I gently nudged the end of the table. The coffee went tumbling, spilling all over the place.

"Oh no." Adeline jumped out of the way.

"I'll clean it up if you don't mind going to get me another one?" I asked hoping she'd take the bait.

"I'll go," Peony chimed right on in with her chipper voice.

"That's okay. Adeline knows exactly where it is and how I like it." I pulled a couple bucks out of my bag and handed it to Adeline. "Get three."

"Sure." Adeline didn't make haste. When I saw she was a couple booths away, I turned to Peony.

"Listen," I warned. "You can't go around talking about spiritualists. I told you that back in Whispering Falls. No one, not even Adeline, knows about our gifts."

"Oh." Peony curled her button nose. "I thought you might have told her since you two are such good friends. And your mom wasn't and she was best friends with Eloise."

"How did you know that?" I asked, knowing not many people knew my history.

"Petunia told Amethyst and Gwenie when I was helping Petunia brush the animals." Peony dragged her finger along the homeopathic cure side of the wall.

Petunia was probably so mad at me, she was telling everything I had ever told her. Even things in confidence. Many times I had even helped her brush the animals after all the shops were closed. The animals loved it as they lined up one by one in her shop. She was good with them and I enjoyed watching her glow when she used her gift.

"I still don't think you had anything to do with Gwenie's death." Peony was again spouting off at the mouth.

I looked around to see if Adeline was anywhere near and let Peony continue to flap her jaws.

"I think Gwenie was still all pissed," Peony stopped, her eyes wide. "I can say pissed right?"

"Sure." I shrugged and haphazardly rearranged some bottles so it looked as if I wasn't paying too much attention to what she was saying, but I was all ears. "Go on."

"Anyway, Petunia hated you from the moment she heard you were going to take over as Village President." Peony picked up a bottle, uncorked it and smelled. "She came home to visit once and told everyone how you weren't a real spiritualist and about how Izzy had found you, bringing you to Whispering Falls. Oh," she clapped her hands, "and when you let the Dark-Siders become part of the community. She freaked on that."

"Really?" I clearly recall her being totally behind me on my changes when I was Village President.

"Yeah, and she said you only changed the one rule that stated families could only have one shop or something like that because you were sleeping with the sheriff." Peony giggled.

"That was to help her so she could marry Gerald." I wondered if Petunia left out that convenient part. Or the fact that Gerald's crazy ex-wife, Ezmeralda, was the one who threatened me with my death. I still shudder at the thought of her threats, which constantly make me look over my shoulder.

"She always called Gwenie. She never called me, but Gwenie told me all about it." Peony tapped her temple. "I also remember her saying there had never been any crime in Whispering Falls until you came to town. Oh," she put her finger in the air, "she also said you ruined her wedding day because you and Oscar got engaged. 'All about June. Everything is always about June,' were her words. And she said she was going to get back at you one way or another."

My jaw dropped. Everything Peony said did happen, but I had no idea Petunia felt that way. I wondered how many other residents of Whispering Falls felt that way. My stomach started to hurt.

"One way or another?" I gasped wondering if Gwenie had wanted to set fire to the shop and get out, only she didn't get out.

"Amethyst said to Gwenie that she was going to keep an eye on you since she opened Full Moon. Gwenie was all over it. That's when she said she had her sudden case of IBS." Peony rolled her eyes.

"Why did you do that?" I asked.

"Do what?" She planted her hand on her hip.

"You rolled your eyes when you mentioned Gwenie and her IBS." I recalled a definite eye roll.

"Did I?" she innocently asked. I nodded my head. "Well," she leaned in as if someone were listening, "she liked to fake the IBS sometimes to get out of things. She wasn't interested in the smudging ceremony, which I think is super cool. She told me she was going to walk around Main Street, but you ended up catching her. Which probably pissed her off more."

"I didn't catch her. You told me she had IBS and I have a great cure for it." At least I could tell her the truth and her not judge me.

"Listen, she's done this before." Peony smiled. "And if you check out her background, you will know she loved to play with fire."

That was a little bit of news I could sink my teeth into.

"I bet she went to set the place on fire and couldn't get out before she passed out." Peony read my mind.

If what Peony said was true, it might completely get me off the hook.

I glanced around to make sure no one was around to hear me. I tugged on Peony's arm, pulling her closer. I whispered, "Amethyst told me she was a Oneircritic."

"A what?" Peony drew back, her ponytail swayed.

"Interpreter of dreams. Her gift." I waved my hands in the air.

"Oh, right." Peony shook her head. "I thought we were talking about the fires."

"Yes, but I have dreams." My eyes shifted. "Nightmares. And they have been about fires lately."

"Do you think Amethyst has been interpreting your dreams and you not know it?" Peony was on to something. "Somehow using them against you?"

"I think you might be right. But in our village, you aren't allowed to read other spiritualists. It's a rule." I sucked in a deep breath, maybe the Order of Elders hadn't given Amethyst a copy of the bylaws. My gut was feeling much better. "What about the autopsy?" I asked.

"That was a joke." She tossed her hands in the air. "Those two sisters. The Karimas. They don't know what they are doing. She didn't get cremated. Her body is still there. Petunia is beside herself."

"What?" This was the second time Peony made my jaw drop. "Why?"

"Something about they needed more time to check out more things. I'm telling you, they aren't going to find anything. It was all Gwenie's doing. Or Amethyst because she's so damn loyal to Petunia. And she said your cures were hokey." She pointed to me. "But you didn't hear all this from me. After all, I would never betray my family. So we went back to the Treesort and Amethyst had all of those chocolate round cakes from Wicked Good Bakery. I guess she made a deal with the bakery to have those in every room each evening as a treat for her guests."

"You mean the June's Gems?" I asked.

"Yes!" She snapped. "Those. Oh my God," Peony gasped. "Didn't Petunia tell us the day we met you that they were named after you? Don't tell anyone I told you or they might do the same thing to me before I get out of here."

Slowly I nodded my head. "Why are you still here?"

"Gerald thought Petunia should be surrounded by family and since I'm the only real family she has here, I'm assuming he meant me." She stared at me. "Petunia is used to getting what she wants so I never question anything when people tell me to do something."

"Are you and Petunia close?" I asked wondering if I could get Peony to do a little inside job for me.

"As close as sisters can be." She shrugged. "She's older than me and we really don't have anything in common other than family. She definitely doesn't have the same genetics since her gift is different than mine. But I love her. And I don't want to see her hurt or issue ill will on anyone."

"Do you have loyalty to her friends, like Amethyst?" I asked, probing a bit deeper. If I could get her to look into Amethyst, I could spend some time with Raven. Not only did I want to question her about her run-in with

Gwenie and the whole tart scene, I wanted to question her on Amethyst buying June's Gems for the Treesort.

"They aren't my friends." Her head cocked to the side, curiosity set on her face. "Why? Something tells me you are going to ask me to do something."

"Something is right." I smiled. "I want you to be the best of friends with Amethyst while you are here, follow her around. Try to figure out why she would want to use June's Gems in her Treesort, especially if they were named after me. Tell her about your dreams and see if she falls for it."

"That's it?" Peony asked like it was no big deal.

"Yeah. For now." I smiled.

"That's easy." She fanned her hand in front of her nose. "Did you use basil in anything?" She pinched her nose together. "I hate basil."

"Not that I can recall." I looked up at the candelabra. It was doing the job it needed to do. I wondered why Adeline didn't notice a smell.

"I'm out of here because that smells terrible." She waved off. "I'll get in touch with you somehow."

I turned and helped the next customer who came into the booth.

Every one of Peony's words was stamped in my mind. I couldn't wait until the end of the day to tell Oscar all this information so he could investigate Gwenie's background. Or I could tell Mac and he could do it for me. Not to mention the fact that Amethyst hated me too.

If midnight was the only time I could get into Whispering Falls, midnight was my witching hour. I had to talk to Raven. Not only about her words with Gwenie, but what she had seen in the dough.

I had forgotten about the June's Gem Raven had put near the cellar steps. Peony gave me two things I could sink my teeth into. Her little bit of gossip and reminding me of the little chocolaty treat I'd left behind when I fled A Charming Cure the night before.

Chapter Twenty

Even though I was worn out from my first day back at the flea market, I had to keep going. Tiredness didn't absolve the fact I was still being looked at as the number one murder suspect of Gwendolyn, though Peony gave me a little hope when she said they weren't ruling out Gwenie's loyalty to her family.

"Loyalty?" I asked out loud and stared into the open space in the shed. I reached in my bag and took out Madame Torres. "Are the random words scrolling around in your ball meant for Gwenie? Did she set fire to the shop?"

The lights in the shed flickered before shutting off. The night had already fallen on Locust Grove and Madame Torres's orange glow was the only light piercing the darkness.

"Well?" I asked as her ball came to life. I set the beaker down. I couldn't ask questions and make potions at the same time when I talked to Madame Torres. She was good at saying things once and forgetting the rest.

Her ball churned, brewing a storm cloud of colors. The words came fast and furious in bright yellow: *loyal, family, potions, animal, angry, jealous, bitter, revenge, Amethyst, evil.*

Sudden darkness. Sudden silence. The beating of my heart pounded in my ears.

"Amethyst. I clearly saw Amethyst. What are you trying to tell me?" I begged Madame Torres, but she was done with the clues. "Fine. Let me see Amethyst." I demanded.

"You know that is against the rules and if the Order of Elders find out. . ." Madame Torres shut up when I put my hand over her ball.

"Now." I didn't hesitate.

I truly should've stayed in my classes at Hidden Hall, A Spiritualist University, but one thing after another piled up on me and I couldn't commit. I had no idea how to read Madame Torres when she gave me my clues.

Everything she said was in my life, everything but bitter and revenge.

Okay, bitter maybe. Yes, I was bitter a bit toward Petunia and her family for making me leave Whispering Falls. Yes I was bitter for them storming up the hill with torches in their hands. But revenge? Never. I would never seek revenge. As all spiritualists know, revenge was never a good tool for our gifts. It muddied the waters and made the spells go all cock-eyed.

The light clicked back on just as a message rang in on my phone. It was Oscar letting me know he was going to be staying in Whispering Falls because Colton was working on the case.

The phone chirped again. It was Peony.

No luck with the June's Gems. BUT! I found a bottle that looks like it might have come from your shop! The ingredients: plantain, calamus root, black thorn, rue, night shade. Does this mean anything?

I reached for the Magical Cures book and thumbed through the ingredients. I didn't recall making a potion with all of those because most of mine contained four or less herbs.

Night shade. My finger stopped when I felt a shock.

"Night shade," I whispered, tapping Madame Torres's ball.

"Night shade," she repeated back, instantly turning purple with a skull and crossbones taking over her ball. "Poison."

"Oh god," I groaned and reached for my phone.

Yes! I need you to keep your phone on you. I'm going to have you meet me later. Can you steal it? My thumbs flew over my keyboard. I had to get the potion in my hands and confront Amethyst. *Plus I might have you give Amethyst a message where she has to meet me. My dream might just come true tonight and I'll expose her.*

Peony responded: *Got it! Can you make it soon? I'm getting a little nervous here.*

Keep your phone on you! I typed, wondering if I should get in touch with Oscar. There wasn't nothing to tell, yet. And I could always get in touch with him when I decided on my plan. If only I knew what the plan was.

All I knew was Amethyst gave Gwenie the poison in a potion, then set my place on fire. But why would she do that to me? Why would she do that to Gwenie or even Petunia?

"Show me Treesort," I said to Madame Torres again.

Madame Torres filled with the inside of Treesort. The fire was roaring. Everyone was there. Colton, Ophelia, Gerald, Faith, the Karimas, everyone. And there was a big display of June's Gems on the table along with food from The Gathering Grove.

"What on earth is going on?" I brought Madame Torres up to my face to see if I could get a better look. "Good girl." I grinned when I saw Peony talking Amethyst's head off.

I put Madame Torres deep in my bag. It was decided. If I was going to go Whispering Falls, it was now or never. Everyone was there and it was time to get some clues on what the hell was going on. And get that potion bottle from Peony.

"Let's go," I instructed Mr. Prince Charming.

He curled up on his toes, arching his back into a tall bridge, reminding me of the yoga class with Adeline.

"No time for yoga tonight," I said to Mr. Prince Charming.

He yawned and didn't make a fuss about being woken up. We got in the Green Machine and set our sights on the edge of Whispering Falls. Just like the night before, I parked the car in the deep wooded area off the road and we made our trek through the trees and into the side lot of Two Sisters and a Funeral.

There was no denying it, the tug at my gut told me to go inside, snoop around. Everyone was at the Treesort and it would be perfect timing. It was like the stars and moon were lining up, only the stars weren't out and the moon was still covered up by clouds. The faint light down the street caught my peripheral vision.

There was a light on at Wicked Good. Gwenie was dead. She wasn't coming back; maybe Raven was at the bakery and she might have some answers I needed. I didn't see her at the Treesort, while I did see her sister Faith. Hopefully Raven was alone.

It wasn't hard to get from the funeral home to Wicked Good. The moon was cast in a shadow, leaving the evil lingering in the air. It was almost hard for me to breathe, but if I was going to get anywhere, tonight was the night.

The back door of Wicked Good was propped open, the music was blaring and flour was flying. Raven shimmied and shook to the music, singing a word here and there as she mixed and stirred her delicious creations.

I gave a light knock on the door, making Raven jump around, throwing raw dough at my face.

"Whoa!" I ducked in time for the weapon to whiz past my head.

"God! June! You scared the crap out of me." Raven pushed her black hair back with the back of her hand. Her face dusted in flour. "Get in here before they come for you." She waved me in and shut the door behind me when I was safely inside. "What are you doing here?"

"Nothing is being done to get me back in town and charges haven't been filed so I need to find answers out for myself." I looked over the counter of the goodies.

"I heard they were going to file a charge against you tomorrow so you had to come back and stay. Something about you having all the fun in Locust Grove not caring a thing about your shop or Gwendolyn." She shook her head.

"You don't think I had anything to do with burning down my own shop, let alone killing Gwenie." I was getting a feeling of disconnect from my friend.

"It's strange how you just up and went back to Locust Grove and started your booth back up, that's all." She shrugged and went back to kneading the ball of dough in front of her.

"I think it's strange you are supplying Amethyst with a product named after me." My eyes lowered. I could feel the heat rising. "Especially after you left me the box of June's Gems on the steps of Mystic Lights cellar last night."

"I did not." Raven turned her face toward me. "I did no such thing."

"Right." I wasn't buying it. "How did they get there?"

"June, I reluctantly made those for Amethyst. A few of her customers told her they loved them. She bought some for the rooms and insisted they be at her big grand opening party tonight. I had to keep her in mind when I was making them because. . ." abruptly she stopped. Her hands deep in the dough. Her words not coming out.

"What?" I asked. When there was no movement from her I knew she saw something in the dough, I begged, "Please tell. I have a right to know."

"I can't." She bit her lip. "I can't break the rules anymore."

"Break the rules? You are my friend. What are you talking about?" I asked.

"Petunia took over as Village President. She put an article in the Whispering Falls Gazette stating Rule Number One was going to be enforced. No spiritualist is allowed to read another one in the community until the investigation of her cousin is over." She gulped.

"She can't do that," I protested.

"She can do what she wants. She's in charge. Maybe you should go." She took her hands out of the dough and walked over to the door, opening it.

"Are you serious?" I asked. "Do you honestly think I did this to my own shop?"

"I think people do strange things when they are up against a wall. But no. I know you didn't do it and we have to figure out who did. In fact, Faith is going around the village asking questions and going to do an exposéeon the murder along with reasons why you wouldn't have done it." Raven walked over and gave me a hug. "I know you didn't do it. I also know there is evil and it will rear it's ugly head. I guarantee you we will all be here standing right behind you when it does."

"You are right! I didn't do it. And I really appreciate everything you do hear or find out because I have a couple theories that I want to keep to myself until I have a couple solid leads." I wanted to blurt out all the things I had learned about Amethyst and the potion, but my gut told me I needed to keep it to myself. What if I was wrong? What if Amethyst wasn't the killer? I had to be sure.

Seconds later, an explosion sent me flying in the air. My bag thrown from my body. Madame Torres rolled out and lit up, bright red flames flickered on her surface. I reached my hand out for her. Something red and sharp dug into my leg. I winced at the pain radiating through my body. The object came down again, I rolled to the right to get out of the way as it pierced the dirt.

Madame Torres was just out of my reach. A picture of The Gathering Rock appeared in her globe.

"Do I need to go to The Gathering Rock?" I asked.

The back door of Wicked Good went up in flames. I covered my head.

"Raven!" I screamed looking back. "Raven!"

Hisss, hisss. The sound turned my eyes back toward Madame Torres.

The yellow snake I had seen at Eloise's curled and wrapped around Madame Torres, dragging her off. The smoky air cleared. Mr. Prince Charming's tail danced a few feet from me. The snake slithered away just in time for the red object to miss him.

"Help me," I gasped reaching out for anything, anyone. Another explosion propelled me forward.

The sound of footsteps ran toward me.

"June!" Oscar's voice echoed through the smoke. Sounds of footprints and voices mixed in his. "Oh God." He sounded desperate.

His hand rubbed my head. He bent down, helping me to my feet. He put my arm around his shoulders, letting me lean against him.

"What are you doing here?" His eyes held disappointment in them. He swept me off my feet and into his arms, running across the street to A Charming Cure.

"Hold it right there, Oscar!" Colton screamed. His footsteps getting closer. "You can't save her this time!"

The sound of fire trucks and emergency vehicles sped down the street, stopping at Wicked Good. Oscar didn't stop. He whisked up into the shop and into the storage room.

"I said stop!" Colton stood at the storage room door. His wand pointing right at us. "I have more experience than you. Hand her over and no charges will be filed against you."

Oscar put my feet on the ground but still held me up.

"Good. Now put her on the ground and walk over here with me." Colton kept his wand and eyes on me.

In a flash, Oscar drew his wand. Smoke and fireworks surrounded us. The next thing I knew, I was in the comfort of Eloise's garden with Oscar by my side.

Chapter Twenty-One

"Madame Torres." I gasped, holding my leg. "She's gone. Some snake took her."

"Forget her. She's not been much help to you now." Oscar bent down and waved his wand over my leg. "Bend your leg."

I did what I was told.

"It worked." I bent my leg a few times. The pain was gone. "You are using your wand."

"That's what night classes can do for a wizard." He laughed, though worry was written all over his face. "Now, what are you doing here?"

"I had to come." I knew he wasn't going to like what I had done. "It seemed no one was getting anywhere with what was going on. The evidence keeps piling up against me. Someone was there tonight. Someone stabbed my leg."

Oscar helped me up to sitting. Eloise came outside.

"What is going on?" she asked. She bent down to get a look at me. "Something evil is here." She moved her head side to side, her eyes darting back and forth. "Get her inside."

Oscar and I didn't hesitate. He got me to my feet and with his help, I put more pressure on my leg. It was feeling much better since he waved his wand over it.

"There is something very, very evil that wants to kill you." Eloise was chopping away at some herbs she had picked from the vines of the tree inside her house. "And I'm not so sure it's not from the mortal world."

"What are you saying?" Oscar stood next to his aunt watching her dice the concoction she was making. "I'm sensing a breach in the system."

"As in a mortal?" I asked, not knowing what any of this meant.

"Yes. I feel someone has figured out who we are and they are using you to help destroy the community. I also feel Madame Torres is safe, so you need to know she will come back to you." Eloise got out her steel ball with the long chain she uses for the nightly cleansing of the streets. "Someone is definitely trying to destroy us and I'm going to walk the streets all night in order to help uncover the intruder."

"Oscar," I put my hand on him. "Do you think Adeline knows?"

"Why? Did you tell her something?" he asked.

"No," I shook my head. "But I was careless. When she helped me with the booth this morning, I didn't really let her help me."

"What did you do?" Oscar was getting good at making me feel bad. "God, June." He ran his hands through his hair.

"Well, when she wasn't looking I sprinkled a potion around the booth to get it set up in a matter of seconds. Everything was done when she got back. She did question it, but took my explanation for what it was worth. Plus when Peony came to see me. . ."

"Peony came to see you?" Eloise asked.

"Yeah, and she's so young and innocent, she doesn't realize the things she says and I had to send Adeline off when Peony was talking about Gwenie's death." I could just kill myself for being so careless. "It's just that I've been around here so long, it's my way of life. I forget not everyone is a spiritualist, especially outside of Whispering Falls."

"What did Adeline say?" Eloise asked.

"Nothing. But Peony had plenty to say." I gulped. "Did you know Gwenie has been in trouble before with fire?" I looked at Oscar. "Plus she wasn't cremated because the Karimas are looking at other ways she might have died."

"She was poisoned," there was regret in his voice. "But there was also some dried blood in her hair. Her skull was pierced with a small object, hitting the brain. They are doing the forensics to see if the blunt force came to the head before or after the poisoning."

"What?" I gasped, nervously tucking a piece of hair behind my ear. I rubbed my head thinking about the object that might have hit her and about the poison Amethyst gave her. "I might have some evidence Amethyst gave her poison." I bit my lip, knowing Oscar would go nuts if he knew I had brought Peony into this mess.

"The Karima sisters finished the autopsy. Colton said Gwendolyn's stomach had three substances in it. The IBS cure you gave her, remnants of June's Gem, and poison." Oscar said. "How do you know about the poison?"

"I sort of asked Peony to look around." I pulled the phone out of my bag and showed him the texts. He showed them to Eloise.

"Gwenie didn't like June's Gem. She even said so, to my face." My eyes lowered. "And Amethyst. She's serving them like they are named after her in her Treesort. None of this is making sense to me. None of it." I stopped. "What if she laced the June's Gems with the poison?" I was grasping for straws. "And her history shows she has been in trouble for fires before."

Things Peony said to me earlier flooded my head.

"Peony said Petunia was mad at me for all sorts of reasons. She was mad because I became Village President, taking it from her. She is mad because Oscar asked me to marry him on her wedding day. She's mad because I'm breathing!" I slammed my fist on the counter.

"Maybe there is more to it and you aren't looking at it from the spiritualist prospective." Eloise opened the ball and stuffed it full with whatever she was making.

"How could you say that?" I asked. "I have all the evidence pointing to Amethyst. We just have to catch her."

"Have you really let your intuition guide you? Madame Torres and Mr. Prince Charming can only take you so far." She warned, "I feel it's only a matter of time before they find you. They are busy now sorting through Wicked Good, asking Raven many questions of why you were there. I believe she's covering for you. But I'm going to walk the streets. You," she pointed at me, "need to get in touch with your spiritual side and let it guide you. Not your head. Not your heart. Not physical evidence."

I gulped. She was right. I was letting my emotions get in the way of my duties.

"You need to stay put." She wasn't letting Oscar off the hook. "Colton will have you locked up in no time for helping her."

"Understood." Oscar took me by the hand and we followed Eloise to the front door. We watched her dart into the night.

"I'm going to lay down for a minute," I said to Oscar.

My leg felt better, but it still ached a little. We walked over to the couch in front of Eloise's fireplace. With a flick of his wand, Oscar lit the logs inside and sat down on the couch, pulling me to him.

"Think back to Adeline and her visits here." Oscar pulled me closer, I laid my head on his shoulder and closed my eyes. "I'm not so sure she isn't the killer. After all, you did put her boyfriend behind bars."

I gulped. It wasn't too long ago, her boyfriend had been convicted, thanks to me. But she was past that. We were past that. Weren't we?

All of Adeline's visit came back to me. There wasn't anything signaling me to her knowing how everything around Whispering Falls worked. She was always a good friend. Never asking questions. Accepting me for who I was.

"No, no," I begged. My weak hands batted at the flames surrounding me. The yellow snake curled his body around my legs. Tighter and tighter. I fought. The grip the snake had on me cut off the circulation to my legs. The red weapon was above me, trying to come down on me like a hammer shattering the tile beneath me. I crawled back on my hands, scooting on my butt, with my back against The Gathering Rock. The snake pulled. The red weapon missed. The yellow serpent pulled again, this time longer, harder. I gasped. I wanted to protest, but my lungs were filled. I could feel my time was coming to an end. The evil one had won. Suddenly, out of nowhere, the killer's feet stood at my head. Red strappy heels.

"No!" I flung my hands in the air. Oscar grabbed them and held me tight. I fought him. He held tighter.

"June, shhh," he whispered into my hair. "You were having a nightmare."

I stopped failing. My chest heaved up and down. Every inch of my skin crawled with fear, anger, and desperation.

"Oscar!" I broke out of his grip. "The snake. The snake was trying to save me. Amethyst. She wears red heels. The weapon is the heel of her shoe."

"Slow down. What snake?" he asked. "Shoes?"

"The snake that was here last night while we were on the gazebo. The yellow snake." I shook my head.

"There was no yellow snake."

"There had to be. The snake saved Madame Torres tonight. The snake is trying to save me. But from whom?" I tried to go back into my memory. "Mystic Lights!" I jumped up. "We have to go to Mystic Lights."

"We aren't going anywhere." He pulled me back down.

"We have to." I broke from him again. "My nightmare," I recalled the red weapon shattering the tile floor. "The next fire is going to happen at Mystic Lights. If I go, you can be in the background and see it's Amethyst for yourself."

"I don't know, June." Oscar shook his head and wrung his hands in front of him. "Aunt Eloise told us to stay put. And if it doesn't work, you and I will both be going to jail for a very long time."

"She also said to follow my intuition. And it's telling me to go to Mystic Lights." I looked around, not knowing which way to head back to town. "And what do we have to lose? We can't hide out the rest of our lives. You and I both know the spiritual world is too powerful not to find us."

Chapter Twenty-Two

Oscar didn't question me when I told him I had to go to A Charming Cure before we went to Mystic Lights. My gut told me Amethyst was written all over it. She was the one who wore red shoes and there was no denying my nightmares showed vividly her red heels.

"Did you get a chance to see the autopsy report?" I asked Oscar.

"Colton did tell me about it." Oscar went ahead of me in the tunnel between Eloise's tree house and my shop. He waved his hands in the dark, clearing the cobwebs. He didn't have the touch like Eloise to light our way, so we went blindly. "Why?"

"Do you think the hole was as big as the bottom of the heel of a woman's high-heeled shoe?" I asked.

"He said it was the size of a bullet. But there was no bullet in her head when they did the autopsy." Oscar took the steps leading up to the shop one by one, making sure I was okay behind him. "I guess a shoe could do it, but the killer would have to be pretty strong."

So maybe my shoe theory could be way off, but it was better than thinking she was poisoned by my IBS cure or a June's Gem.

"But if she was poisoned by a June's Gem, then maybe. . ." I shudder to think about the truth of what I was about to say. "Someone left me a box of June's Gems at the steps of the cellar. Raven said it wasn't her. She was also at the other end of Gwenie's distaste. Raven is a Dark-Sider and she doesn't take criticism too well." I gulped and took Oscar's hand as he helped me out of the underground path and into the storage room of A Charming Cure. "Do you think Raven's Dark-Sider ways have come back?" I asked, remembering how bitter and angry Raven was when I met her when I attended Hidden Halls, A Spiritualist University.

"I don't know." Oscar shut the trap door and moved the rug back over top it. "You and I both know that anything is possible around here."

There was no time to spare.

"Can you go to the window and make sure the moon is still full?" I asked Oscar.

He didn't hesitate. He rushed to the window and pulled back the curtain. I went to my shelf of ingredients.

"The lights of Glorybee are on," Oscar said. "It looks like Amethyst and Petunia are in there."

"Good. I need her to see us when we walk over to Mystic Lights." I couldn't have planned it any better.

"Just like that. We are going to walk across the street?"

"Yes." I sucked in a deep breath and continued touching the bottles one by one. "Slippery elm, adder's tongue, cloves, drawing powder and," my finger glided across the bottles as I plucked what I needed, "agate stone."

I set the bottles down next to the cauldron and flipped it on.

"Is it full?" I asked uncorking all the ingredients. In order to get my potion of truth serum to work, a full moon was best. Not that I didn't believe in my spells, but having a little extra oomph wasn't going to hurt.

"Yes." Oscar's voice escalated. "Yes. It's a full moon."

"Great." I grabbed the agate rock and placed it in the bottom of the cauldron. "Can you come over here and help me?"

He rushed over. "What can I do?"

"You pick up both of those bottles," I instructed him and I had the other two in my hands. "On the count of three, dump them in at the same time."

"Okay." He was focused on the cauldron. The agate stone was already smoking, waiting for the ingredients to do their thing.

"One, two," I said as Oscar squeezed his eyes shut, "three."

Together, we poured in the entire contents of all four bottles on top of the stone. The ingredients swirled and twirled. Oscar barely opened his eyes, just enough to see what was going on.

"Shoo." His eyes opened wide. "I thought it might be another blast."

"No." I pointed to the ladle. He handed it to me. "This is a truth serum. I'm going to stick it into a June's Gem and when we go to Mystic Lights, I'm giving it to Amethyst. I know she is going to be there. I can feel it."

"I sure hope you are right because if you aren't. . ."

I put my finger up to Oscar's mouth.

"I am." There was confidence in my words. She had to be there. I was counting on it.

Slowly I stirred the mixture. The bubbling, glowing, viscous mixture was black, but glowed crimson. I continued to picture Amethyst in my mind. Basil scent curled into the steam, knotting my stomach. Basil was the sure sign evil was lurking.

The cauldron shut off, letting me know it was ready. I reached on the counter for the box of June's Gems that were left at the cellar steps. They had to be from Amethyst. Was it her calling card? I wondered.

Using the end of the ladle, I made a small hole in the bottom of each June's Gem. I inserted just enough of the truth serum to get a confession. I replaced the hole with the icing, using my finger to smooth it back over.

"How do you know to do all of this?" Oscar leaned on the counter. Amazement in his eyes.

"I have no idea," I said, which wasn't a lie. "I'm doing what Eloise said. Rely on your gift. My intuition."

"I hope it works." He shook his head.

"Stop saying that." I replaced the June's Gems in the box and shut the lid. "Are you ready?"

"As I will ever be." Oscar put his hand out for me to take. I did. He squeezed it. Our eyes met. It was time. We were going to do this together and it felt right.

Before we left, I grabbed my phone and texted Peony.

It looks like Amethyst is at Glorybee. Can you meet me at The Gathering Rock in about twenty minutes with the bottle? I'm going to draw her there and expose her!

Peony quickly sent back: *I will be there. Twenty minutes!*

Yes. I texted her back. *I'm heading over to Mystic Lights and will lure her to the rock.*

I put my phone back in my bag and stood at the door.

"Are you ready?" I asked Oscar.

He responded with a big kiss.

The old air swooped in around us when we opened the door. My adrenaline was pumping and not even the cold air was going to stop me.

My cloak edges dragged the pavement. The wind howled through the empty tree branches. Oscar's footsteps echoed down Main Street.

"June!" Petunia called out under the full moon. "June!"

Oscar's hand squeezed mine. We kept our eyes forward and headed up the steps of Mystic Lights. The door was slightly ajar. We paused, looking at each other.

"It's a sign." I gulped. "She's in there."

In the blink of an eye, the explosion happened before we could step inside. Through the smoke, the red heel of a woman's shoe came hammering down between us. I knew it had hit Oscar when his hand went limp in mine.

I ran to the back of the shop where Izzy's office was, cradling the box of June's Gems. I looked back. The killer must have held a potion for the explosion and threw it at us because the shop was not on fire.

"June! Come out!" I heard Petunia call into the shop.

One of Izzy's crystal balls lit up. Colton was out front helping Oscar to his feet. Oscar was rubbing his head. He was okay, but I was in here. Another crystal ball showed Raven in her shop looking over the damage of the fire. While another one showed Amethyst back at her Treesort putting out more June's Gems.

Anger boiled in me. If my plan for her to come to me was not going to work, I was going to her.

Before I knew it, I ran down the basement steps and through the cellar door in order to escape from anyone seeing me. I ran around the backs of the shops and when the shadow of the clouds slid over the moonlight, I crossed the street.

I took a quick glance down Main Street and focused on the front steps of Mystic Lights. Oscar was sitting up and talking to Colton. If he was okay, I could continue on with the plan. Petunia was also standing near them.

I scurried up the hill, stopping at The Gathering Rock to catch my breath.

"June? Is that you?" Peony walked out of the woods. "Oh my God." She hurried over. "Are you okay?"

"I'm fine." I assured her. "Did you bring the potion?"

"Yes. And I think you are right about Amethyst." Her eyes filled with tears. "I just saw her run to Treesort after something exploded. She must be running away so no one saw her."

The smell of basil filled the midnight air. I slid down The Gathering Rock. I put my hand on the ground. My mind went dizzy and the air thinned. Out of the corner of my eye, the yellow snake slithered down the hill toward Whispering Falls.

My eyes slid toward Peony. I couldn't focus as she rambled on and on about why she thought Amethyst was the killer.

"Are you okay?" She sat down next to me. Her long dress swooshed around her. In a quick second, I could see the red shoes she was wearing. "You don't look so good."

"Can you hand me the box?" I asked reaching for the box from Wicked Good. "I'm diabetic and I need a small pinch." I lied.

Peony didn't waste a second. She opened the box.

"You can have one too," I sounded like I was exhausted. "I have to have my strength in order to confront Amethyst."

Peony picked up a June's Gem. She held it toward me. Then stopped. She took a big bite. I closed my eyes when my breath was suddenly taken out of my lungs. My eyes opened, focusing on Peony's shoes.

She followed my eyes and looked down. The tips of her shoes were sticking out from underneath her long dress.

"So," she adjusted her dress to cover up the shoes. "You are diabetic?"

"Yes. I need just a pinch." I lied. She knew I saw her shoes. My gut told me. "If you don't give me a bite, I can die." I reached toward her and she shifted backward.

"You know and I know I can't give you a bite." She lifted the chocolaty cake back to her lips and sunk her teeth deep into it, taking in the truth serum. "I would have if you hadn't seen my shoes, but I just can't take the risk now."

"Why? Why did you do it?" I asked, acting as though I were about to pass out.

"It doesn't matter. My lips are sealed." She grinned. "Help! June is going to kill me! Help!" She screamed over her shoulder. Her shrill voice echoed down the hill. "I've got her up here!"

She slipped off her shoes.

"What are you doing?" I was trying to buy time. I didn't know how long it took for the potion to kick in. But the moon was full and the fireflies were going nuts, surely to goodness it had to take effect soon.

She lifted her hand in the air, just like I had seen in my nightmare. I covered my head. She was going to kill me like she did Gwenie.

"What?" She laughed. "You think I'm going to whack you in the head like I did Gwenie?" Her laughter echoed. "I'm going to give you my shoes and I'm going to take yours. Gwenie was supposed to burn up after I whacked her in the head." She cackled putting her hand over her mouth. "Oops. I let that one slip."

"So you did kill her?" My eyes lowered. The cast of a shadow was walking up the hill.

"Shhh." She put her finger up to her lips. "Do you hear that? Someone is coming." She took the bottom of her shoe and whacked herself in the head. Blood trickled down her temples. She grinned. She let out a blood-curdling scream, "Hurry! She just hit me!"

The shadow stopped and stepped into the light. Petunia had Madame Torres in the palm of her hand and the yellow snake was coiled around her body. Once we made eye contact, she slipped back into the shadow.

"Why? Why would you kill Gwendolyn?" I asked.

"Are you kidding me?" Her words were sharp, angry. "I could never be the sister Petunia wanted me to be. You should know how that is, being the outsider. All this magical gift crap. Well guess what?" The truth potion kicked in. "I'm not a spiritualist. My family was a lot like yours. My mom was like sweet animal whisperer

Petunia. And my father was a non-spiritualist. Lucky me.
I got the crappy genes."

I groaned, for good measure, and lifted myself
straighter up against the rock.

"It was perfect. Our precious little Gwenie made
sure to let me know I was not one of them. Oh I tried
being a good sister when Petunia would complain about
you. Your slipping in here becoming Village President,
ruining her engagement, being so beautiful. And I used it
to my advantage. You were the perfect target for me to
feed crap to Gwenie. She would protect Petunia at all
costs." She rubbed the blood from the corner of her lips.
"What is taking these idiots so long to get up here?"

"How did you do it?" I asked biding time, wondering
why Petunia wasn't stepping in to help me.

"I had to make myself blend in. Gwenie and Petunia
know I'm not a spiritualist. Amethyst doesn't. But my
family knew, which made them want to include me in on
everything." She looked back down the hill and turned
back to me.

Everything was making sense. All the times I had to correct her for speaking about the magical happenings around Adeline and when she was at the shop and how she used a watchful eye while I was making the potions when the shop was closed.

"I still don't understand why you did it. Why did you kill her? Why did you want to create havoc?" I asked.

"June, you aren't very smart." Peony's cheeks balled with an evil grin. "I was so sick of playing the outcast of the family. Petunia needed to lean on me. Not a cousin. When I found out she was going to become the Village President, I wanted to be the one to help her. I wanted to give her a makeover, move here and be of some assistance." Her smile faded from her face. She curled her nose, and squinted her eyes. The blood continued to trickle down her temple. "Gwenie told me I was delusional. She said my sister would never pick me because I'm not a spiritualist. I was a nobody. A loser." She threw her head back and laughed. "Look who the loser is now. Her and you. You were the perfect person to frame. Petunia had many reasons to hate you. Since

she and Gwenie were so close and Gwenie made my job
easy by putting you down, it was hands down a no
brainer."

She had a satisfied look on her face.

"You won't get away with this." I glared at her.

She looked back. The sound of footsteps were
climbing the hill.

"Hurry! She's going to kill me like she did Gwenie!"
Peony couldn't keep a straight face as she screamed
toward the hill.

The yellow snake slithered around The Gathering
Rock and curled around her feet, sending her to the
ground.

"What in the hell?" Peony fought against the snake
as the snake contorted itself like a coil all the way up and
around Peony, stopping as their eyes came face to face.
Peony stared. Fear darted out of her eyes.

"We've heard enough." Petunia slipped out of the
forest. Madame Torres appeared inside her ball. Her
flaming red hair and lips lit up like the fires Peony had
started.

"Get this thing off me, sister." Peony spit.

"That is our dear sweet cousin Gwendolyn. When the autopsy report came back that something blunt, like your shoe, killed her, she couldn't be cremated right away." Petunia jutted her hand toward me and helped me up. "A little known spiritualist secret," Petunia bent down, nose to nose with her sister. "People can come back as animals." She threw her head back and cackled into the night sky. "I'm an animal whisperer, so of course Gwenie here," she stroked the yellow snake, "came to visit me, letting me in on the dirty little secret of how jealous you are of me and the spiritual world."

"Dear sister, it was her." Peony scowled. "June Heal hates you! She took your presidency away from you! She got engaged on your wedding day taking the spotlight off of you!"

"Enough!" Petunia screamed.

Colton and Oscar raced up the hill.

"Arrest her!" Petunia pointed toward her sister. "For the death of Gwendolyn Shrubwood and arson."

"Sister! How could you?" Peony fought against Gwenie as she slithered off of her and Colton grabbed her wrists. "I did this for the love of the family."

"You never loved our family," Petunia spit.

Gwenie slid her way around the rock and next to me. She curled into a neat pyramid, coming face to face with me. If she weren't a snake, I'd swear she smiled at me. I patted her on the head.

"Are you okay?" Oscar hurried over to me and took me in his arms. "I was so scared when you went rushing into Mystic Lights."

"Did she ruin the shop?" I couldn't bare another store in Whispering Falls going up in flames.

"She's a rookie." Colton said, tightening the cuffs on Peony's wrists. She shrugged her shoulder forward, trying to tug away. "She made some little homemade Molotov cocktail that only exploded in front of her after she threw it creating smoke around her as if she were a spiritualist."

"I did it for the good of my family." Peony twisted left and right before Colton put a tighter grip on her.

Raven ran up the hill. "It's her!" She pointed to Peony. She had a lump of dough in her hands. "Oh." Relief settled on her face. "You have her." She held the dough up. By the light of the moon, there was a red heel in the dough. "She wanted everyone to think it was June. On her way to Gwendolyn's cremation, she stopped in and got a box of Gems saying Petunia wanted them for the midnight ceremony. I didn't think twice about it until June thanked me for the box she found on the steps of Mystic Light's cellar."

"It was perfect to get June to Wicked Good and fight with you so I could set your shop on fire and making it look like she did it." Peony sang like a bird. The truth serum had completely kicked in.

"Aren't you so forth-coming." Colton dragged her down the hill.

"The truth serum?" Oscar grinned. His beautiful teeth gleamed in the moonlight.

"Yes. I thought it was going to be for Amethyst. I had no idea it was Peony until I saw her shoes. Over and over in my nightmare I saw something red come down as the weapon." I pointed to the shoes lying by the rock. "She was going to stick them on my feet to try to frame me one last time."

"I'm so sorry, June." Petunia walked over, the fireflies darted in and out of her hair. "I really didn't know what to think until Gwenie came to me." She put her arms out and let Gwenie coil around them, resting her head on Petunia's shoulder. "She told me everything. I had to wait until I became Village President to stop her. Gwenie told me your plans of coming to Mystic Lights. At midnight last night, I knew I was the president and told Amethyst everything. We pulled Constance Karima aside and explained to her how Gwenie couldn't be cremated because she had come back as the snake. I couldn't let my sister get away with it."

"Please don't apologize." I put my arms around her and they hugged me back. "You have to know I would never have hurt you."

She waved me off.

"There is no need to apologize." She ran her hand down my arm. "You have made Whispering Falls a thriving community. You add to the village."

Oscar walked over and put his arms around me. Silently we watched Colton take Peony down the hill, across the street and into the station where she would be held until the Order of Elders came for her, taking her wherever they took the criminals.

Since Peony was not a spiritualist, I wasn't sure where she would go and I didn't care. As long as she was far away from me and my family.

"Are you okay?" Oscar asked.

"I'm fine," I assured him.

I walked over and picked up Madame Torres where Petunia had left her.

I rubbed her ball and held her close to me. Mr. Prince Charming darted out from the woods and did figure eights around my ankles.

"I'm great. Perfect." A wave of satisfaction swept over me.

I might not have a biological family and it was okay. The family I had was right here in Whispering Falls. My community had become my family.

Chapter Twenty-Three

Ding, ding. The bell over the door of A Charming Cure jiggled back and forth letting me know someone was here.

"I'll be right with you," I called out from behind the partition. I had spent all night at the cauldron trying to play catch up from the last week.

After the whole thing with Peony, Amethyst hosted a congratulations party for Petunia and it was a big blow out. She had food from The Gathering Grove along with desserts from Wicked Good. There was even a band she had come up from her old village in Florida. They played all night and it was the first time Oscar and I had danced, and we did all night long.

The days after the party, Petunia took her rightful spot as the Village President, holding an emergency meeting to cleanse the village from the evil that had lurked there. She even made peace with her sister, Peony, though Peony was going to be locked up for the rest of her life for the death of their cousin. Petunia was so kind-hearted.

The Order of Elders had our spiritual construction crew fix the doors of Wicked Good and Mystic Lights. That didn't take them any time, but the roof of my shop took a day. It was perfect and brand new like nothing had ever happened.

I had a lot of potions to get on the shelf and I had spent all night getting them done.

"Petunia." I was happy to see my friend standing near the door. I rubbed my hands down my apron to clean off any residue from the cauldron and walked from behind the counter. "I'm so glad to see you."

Mr. Prince Charming jumped off the counter, following me across the room. He did his signature figure-eight move around her ankles until she finally picked him up, a few dried leaves falling from her hair onto my floor.

There was a box sitting next to her feet.

"I wanted to stop by before the morning rush." She rubbed down Mr. Prince Charming's fur. He purred with delight. "I have a little grand opening surprise for you."

"Grand opening?" My head tilted.

The sound of hammers came from outside my shop. I moved over to the window. Gerald was waving his hand to the right giving instructions to Oscar and Colton, who were on ladders on each side of my wisteria vine.

"To the right!" Gerald waved his hand. "More, more," he instructed them. He threw his hands in the stop position. "Right there!"

The hammering started again.

"The village wanted to do something nice for you since we were all a little yucky with the whole fire and death of my cousin." Her words were sincere and quiet. "You really never had a Grand Opening of the shop and now with a new roof it's kind of like a new opening. Plus I thought you could use a new cauldron with how great the shop has been doing." She used the toe of her black lace-up boots and tapped the box on the floor. "We used a little bit of the village fund to get you a new cauldron. It's supposed to be the latest and greatest."

"Oh!" My heart filled with joy. I flung my arms around her, Mr. Prince Charming jumped down, growling the entire time he dashed under the red tablecloth of one of the display tables. "You didn't have to do that, but thank you so much."

"No." She hugged me back. I had to tilt my head to the left so the bird's tail feather sticking out from her messy updo didn't poke me in the eye. "I owe you a big apology." She pulled away. Her eyes stared at me. Her face stilled. "I should have never led the lynching mob up the hill. I was upset and angry. I knew in my gut you didn't or couldn't hurt a flea and you are my friend. But I needed to blame someone for the pain I was feeling. I'm sorry, June. I really am."

"Oh stop," I used my hand to shoo her. "You don't need to apologize. I know your heart. Thank you." I bent down to look at the box. "You really didn't need to do this."

"From what your Aunt Helena tells me, it's the best." She stood with pride on her face.

"You went to Wands, Potions and Beyond?" I was shocked Petunia left Whispering Falls for Hidden Halls, A Spiritualist University where the magic shop was located.

"I did. And you know," she leaned in. "Don't tell Gerald, but I couldn't help but look at the baby section." She pulled back grinning from ear-to-ear.

"Are you telling me you are?" I questioned hesitantly and pointed at her mid-section.

"Maybe." She winked and headed out the door. I followed.

Oscar, Colton, and Gerald stood on the sidewalk looking at the big Re-Grand Opening banner they had hammered over the shop door.

Cough, cough, "What!?" Gerald picked up Petunia and twirled her around and around. Her long black dress flared out with each spin. He stopped, pulling her into a cradle in his arms, taking off in the direction of Glorybee.

"What was that about? Is everything okay?" Oscar asked.

"Everything is great. All is good with the village." I smiled. "Thank you."

"You are welcome," Colton and Oscar said in sync.

Colton headed across the street.

Oscar's hand slid in the space between us and I grabbed it. We stood there for a while looking at the outside of the shop and the banner.

Life was good. Whispering Falls was great. And we were going to be able to add a plus one to the population in nine months.

Enjoy the first chapter in Tonya's bestselling Laurel London Mystery Series from the first book Checkered Crime.

Chapter One

"Thank God you're here," I hollered to Derek Smitherman who had his head stuck under the hood of a car, his usual position. I slammed the door of the old VW van. "Thanks for lunch." I waved off the guy I had hitched a ride with after our lunch date.

I adjusted my black wrap dress so it was wrapped in all the right places.

Contorting his body, Derek stood up and turned around. He took the dirty oily rag from the back pocket of his blue mechanic overalls and wiped his hands, leaving some smudging on them. He pushed the large-frame black glasses up on the bridge of his nose.

It was a shame he covered up that body; I bet every single woman in Walnut Grove, Kentucky would take their car to him for all of their repairs if he wore a white v-neck t-shirt and a pair of snug Wranglers. Most of the time women got lost in his steel-blue eyes, so bright against his black hair. But if they only knew what was underneath all the clothes...

For years Derek and I used to go skinny dipping in the river until one day our stares lingered a little too long, and we realized our bodies where no longer those of little kids. Derek had grown into a hot dude right before my eyes and I never saw it coming. Too bad I could only think of him like a brother.

"I need your help." I stuck my hands out to the side like I was on a balance beam, trying to keep my five-foot-eight frame upright on my high-heels because the loose pieces of the beat-up concrete walkway made me a little wobbly. I grabbed the lanyard from around my neck with my Porty Morty's ID stuck in the clear pouch and threw it in my bag. "I'm not going to need that any time soon. What about that help?"

I hopped onto a piece of concrete slab that was mostly intact, once again having to readjust the wrap dress.

"I learned my lesson a long time ago that before I agree to help you with anything that I better have all the details of what it is you want." His brows frowned, his eyes narrowed. "Every single detail."

"Simple. I need a car." I took the toe of my heel and batted around a piece of loose concrete to avoid all of the questions that were going to follow.

"No way, no how am I going to help you out." Derek looked over my shoulder at the beat-up van. His five o'clock shadow was a little thicker than normal.

The gears grinded before the driver of the VW gave us the peace sign and took off.

I took a couple steps forward and rubbed the back of my hand down his chin.

"No wonder you can't get any ladies. Clean yourself up." I messed up his hair.

He jerked his head back. He quirked his eyebrow questioningly.

"Who was that?" He asked in a "good ole boy" voice and jerked his head to the right, getting a better view of the VW.

"Gary. . .um. . .Barry I think." I shrugged off his interrogation. "Lunch Date Dot Com."

"Good grief." Derek shook his head. "I'd rather stay single."

Lunch Date Dot Com was a dating website where you met for lunch on your lunch breaks. I didn't even bother to read the guy's profile before I accepted his lunch offer because I was starving and I needed a ride to come out here and see Derek.

"So what about that car?" I wiggled my brows that were in desperate need of a wax.

Given my current money status, I was going to have to settle for Trixie's hot pink jeweled tweezers she picked up on her weekly run to the Dollar Store.

"I don't think so." Derek resumed his position under the hood of the elevated car. "Besides, where is your company car from Porty Morty's?"

"I got fired," I murmured. I adjusted the tight black Diane Von Furstenberg dress I had picked up from the local Salvation Army. Wrapping a piece of my shoulder-length honey-colored hair behind my ear, I batted my grey eyes and used fifteen hundred dollars cash to fan my face. "I've got fifteen hundred dollars. You can use it to fix that little concrete problem you have." I pointed to the chipped-up material.

"Laurel London, did you say fired?" Derek swiftly turned back around and waved a wrench in the air until he saw the cash. There was a little twinkle in his eye. I knew Derek like the back of my hand. He loved cash just as much as I did.

I waved the dough under his nose. "That is why I need a new car."

When I heard a faint sniff as the cash passed his left nostril, I knew he was on the line. It was time for me to hook him and reel him in.

"Trixie will skin my hide if I take that stolen cash."

"Stolen?" Okay. I was officially offended. "You think I stole this money? I want you to know," I jerked my shoulders back and cocked my chin in the air. His eyes were on the cash. "This is guilt money from Morty.

That no good sonofa…," I muttered a few curse words under my breath.

"See, why do you have to go around talking like that?" Derek asked. His face contorted. "That along with your…um…sticky fingers don't make me want to do any sort of favors for you anymore."

"Sticky fingers? Geesh." I threw my hands in the air. "When is this town ever going to get over that?"

"Over it?" He laughed. "Over it?"

"Yeah, heard you the first time." I spoke softly and narrowed my eyes.

"You have pick-pocketed every single person in the town, not to mention how you hacked into the Wilsons' accounts after they took you in."

"Oh that. Phish!" I gestured. "That was seven years ago. I was fifteen years old. Besides, it wasn't like you weren't right there with me." I tapped my temple and then brushed a strand of my hair behind my ear and again fanned myself with the money. Clearly the sticky, humid weather wasn't doing me any favors. "I clearly remember you threading the fishing line on the Quantum Rod and Reel you had on your Christmas list. I played Santa, that's all." I shrugged, recalling all the crappy Christmas presents the orphanage gave all of us year after year and when I had decided to use the Wilsons' credit card to buy all the orphans real Christmas presents.

"It was your chance to get out of the big house and you blew it." Derek shook his head. He put the wrench in his back pocket and crossed his arms in front of him. "Anyone would have given their arm to get out of there and have a real Christmas for once."

True, true. I didn't have a leg to stand on with his argument.

I admired Derek. He got out of the orphanage with a great job and was working on his dream to become a police officer. He was almost finished with night classes at the University of Louisville.

"You didn't tell me the truth about those Christmas presents or I would've never shown up to meet you." Derek's lip turned up in an Elvis kind of way exposing a small portion of his pearly white teeth and deepening the dimple on his cheek. A distant twinkle flickered in his blue eyes. "You sure were believable when you told me they bought all the presents for the orphanage. Genius in fact." He pointed his finger at me. "I credit you for me wanting to be a cop. Since I know how you work, I'm going to be able to figure out how criminal minds work."

"Ha, ha." I slowly clapped my hands. "Very funny," I sneered.

"That was then." I waved the money again. "Before I made myself an honest girl and got a big girl job."

"Getting fired from Porty Morty's is a big girl job?" Derek chuckled. "How did you get fired from selling port-a-lets?"

I wasn't sure, but I detected a little hint of sarcasm in his tone.

"Morty let me go. Something about overhead and people aren't using port-a-potties anymore." My mouth dipped down.

"Where are the people pooping?" Derek's nose curled up.

"Got me." I shrugged. "Anyway, I need a set of wheels. That old 1977 beat-up Caddy was Morty's. He let me borrow it because my job was to get all of those outdoor venues to use Porty Morty's at their events. He made me give it back. I need a new set of wheels to find a job before Trixie finds out. She is going to kill me when I tell her Morty let me go."

Kill might be a strong word to use, but she wasn't going to be happy. Trixie had been in charge of the orphanage for years. It just so happened that when I turned eighteen, the state shut down the orphanage forcing Trixie to retire.

She said I needed guidance and in no formal sort of way she became my guardian. The only mother figure I'd known. In truth, I think she was really worried about me and wanted to make sure I did well. She was the first person to ever see potential in me. Then and there I'd decided I was going to make something of myself. She got me the job with Morty and I'd been working there ever since, bringing home a steady paycheck. Not much. But it was reliable. I was able to get a studio apartment, though my rent was always a tad bit late.

"I love you like a sis' and all, but how am I going to do that?"

"You got all those cars out there." I pointed to the field filled with abandoned cars that Derek used for parts. The grass had grown up around the tires which were probably dry-rotted, and they all had a little rust. Nothing a set of new tires and paint job couldn't fix.

"Those old clunkers? Nah, I don't have anything that's reliable and good enough to drive." He bit the side of his lip.

I waved the money again. "Morty called it compensation." Compensation my ass. It was guilt money. "It's all I have to get me a car. Come on. I've been on the straight and narrow for five years. You know it, and I know it. All I need is a car to get around so I can get another job."

Jobs were slim pickings in our little town of twelve hundred. Louisville was only thirty minutes away and surely I could score some sort of job there.

"I don't know." Derek shook his head. "There really isn't anything out there that fifteen hundred will fix."

I put my hand up to my brows to cover the sun beaming down and scanned the field. There had to be something.

"What about that one?" I pointed to the black-and-white-colored one to the far right. Sort of off by itself.

"That old '62 Plymouth Belvedere?" Derek laughed so hard, he was hyperventilating.

"Yeah. What's wrong with it?" There was no humor in my voice. "Other than the faded sign on the side."

"Come on." He tugged his head to the side. "The engine may need a good clean up."

"Okay." Like I knew what that meant. I followed him to the edge of the grass and stopped to take my shoes off. The heels would've gotten stuck in the ground and I had to keep them clean. It was going to be a long time before I bought any new shoes. "Oh." My face contorted. Up close I could tell the old Belvedere had seen better days.

I swiped my hand across the dusty old door.

"Taxi?" I laughed, never recalling a taxi service in Walnut Grove.

"I got that when the police academy tore down the old building on the edge of town." He pointed to me. Derek was also training to be a deputy with the sheriff's department. On Monday and Wednesday he drove to the University of Louisville for the police academy. "Remember? I told you about how they had us running around the old building and things popped out at us and we had to assess the situation before we pulled the trigger."

Vaguely I remember him saying something about it.

"Still. I'm serious, Derek. I need a ride." I tapped the car. "Even if it does say taxi."

"Can you imagine if you drove that thing down Main Street." He slapped his knee. "Everyone would know you were crazy, not just wonder."

"We could repaint it," I suggested.

"We? We?" He gestured between the two of us. "You mean me."

"Come on," I begged. "You are my only hope of not letting Trixie down. You don't want to do that, do you? After she has done for us. This place." I pointed to his garage.

Trixie owned the property and when Derek graduated from mechanic school, she gave him the run-down building that he had turned into his business.

"Oh." He shook his finger at me. "You are good at playing the guilt card. I worked hard for this place. I went to work every morning before school and every day after school."

"Yeah, but Trixie gave you the car to do it." I reminded him of her other good deed.

His chest heaved up and down as he let out a heavy sigh. He knew I had him.

"The only real problem with it is the rust." He rubbed his hands along the side of the car and walked back to the bumper. "It was garage kept and it has low mileage. I probably should have covered it with a tarp or something, but I thought I'd be using it for parts. I suppose it would look fine if you painted it."

"You can do that for me right?" I squinted to keep the sun out of my eyes. The skies were blue and the sun was bright.

"No. I don't do paint," he protested.

"I bet you could." I tilted my head around the edge of the car to see the other side.

"Laurel, you exhaust me." He bit the side of his lip.

I could tell he was thinking about it so I put the unexplained shadow behind me and batted my lashes. I put my hands together in a little praying way and mouthed please.

"Fine." He jammed his hands in the pockets of his overalls. "It's not going to be perfect," he warned.

"I don't care." I smiled from ear to ear. I held the money out in front of me.

"Nope. I'm not taking the only money you have." He shoved my hand back toward me. "Consider it an early Christmas gift."

"You do love me." I jumped up and down before throwing my arms around his neck.

"No. I love that Quantum Rod and Reel still." He gave me a slight hug back.

About The Author

Tonya has written over 15 novels and 4 novellas, all of which have graced numerous bestseller lists including USA Today. Her novels have garnered over ten national award making her an International Bestseller.

Best known for stories charged with emotion and humor, and filled with flawed characters, her novels have garnered reader praise and glowing critical reviews. She lives with her husband, three teenage boys, two very spoiled schnauzers and one ex-stray cat in Northern Kentucky and grew up in Nicholasville. Now that her boys are teenagers, Tonya writes full time but can be found at all of her guys high school games with a pencil and paper in hand. Come on over and FAN Tonya on Goodreads.

Praise for Tonya Kappes

"Full of wit, humor and colorful characters, Tonya Kappes delivers a fun, fast-paced story that will leave you hooked!" Bestselling Author, Jane Porter

"Fun, fresh, and flirty, Carpe Bead 'Em is the perfect read on a hot summer day. Tonya Kappes' voice shines in her debut novel." Author Heather Webber

"I loved how Tonya Kappes was able to bring her characters to life." Coffee Table Reviews

"With laugh out loud scenes and can't put it down suspense A Charming Crime is the perfect read for summer you get a little bit of everything but romance." Forgetthehousework blog

Edition: October 2014

Copyright © by Tonya Kappes

Editor: Cyndy Ranzau

Made in the USA
Lexington, KY
17 October 2014